I0760481

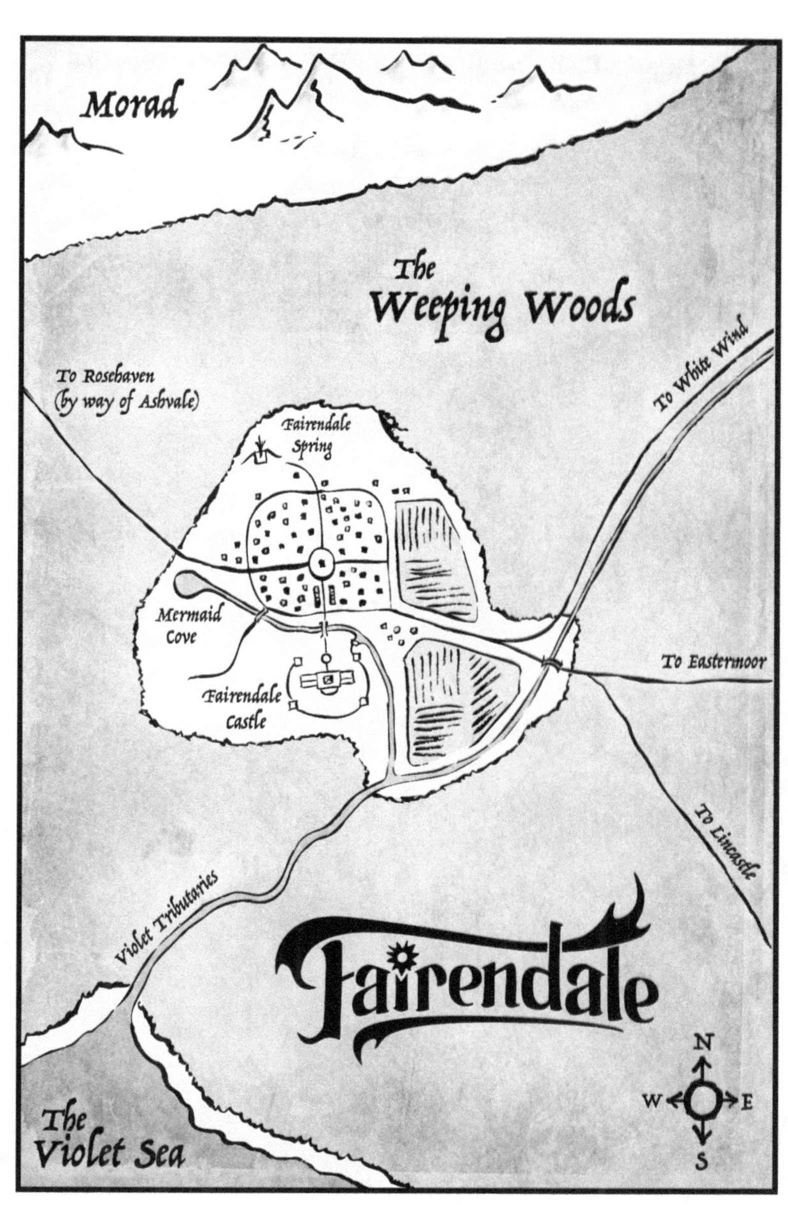
Morad
The Weeping Woods
To Rosehaven
(by way of Ashvale)
Fairendale
Spring
To White Wind
Mermaid
Cove
Fairendale
Castle
To Eastermoor
To Lincastle
Violet Tributaries
Fairendale
N
W
E
S
The
Violet Sea

## Read all the books in the Fairendale series!

Book .5: *The Good King's Fall (a prequel)*
Book 1: *The Treacherous Secret*
Book 2: *The King's Pursuit*
Book 3: *The Perilous Crossing*
Book 4: *The Dragons of Morad*
Book 5: *The Fiery Aftermath*
Book 6: *The Mysterious Separation*

**Collector's Editions:**
Books 1-6: *The Flight of the Magical Children*

**To see all the books L.R. Patton has written, please click or visit the link below:**
www.lrpatton.com/store

Fairendale
1
THE
TREACHEROUS
SECRET

Batlee Press
PO Box 591596
San Antonio, TX 78259

 I appreciate your taking the time to read my work. Please consider leaving a review wherever you bought it, or telling your friends how much you enjoyed it. Both of those help spread the word, which is incredibly important for authors. Thank you for supporting my work.
www.lrpatton.com



Printed in the United States of America

First Edition—2016/Cover designed by Toalson Marketing
www.toalsonmarketing.com

L.R. PATTON

# THE TREACHEROUS SECRET

BATLEE
PRESS

*To my mom,*
*who taught me*
*the power of*
*fairy tales.*

# Beginning

If one were to visit the kingdom of Fairendale, it would take quite an extraordinary mind to imagine what loveliness it wore once upon a time.

This is the land all fairy tales wish they could inhabit. It is the kingdom where the Violet Sea lends its tributaries with grace and generosity, where mermaids wait just below the shallow waters to call out to those brave enough to cross their bridge from the village of Fairendale to the kingdom grounds, where colors of every hue shimmer in the great green grass and the brilliant blue sky and the lacy flowers of orange and yellow and scarlet.

The kingdom, as it used to exist, lived in a perpetual fall, that season of crisp, cool air whispering in ears and stroking cheeks and sneaking into bedroom windows to lie beside sleeping children. Now the wind is hard and biting and bitter, as if anger blows across this land. And anger is certainly justified in its blowing, as we shall soon see.

It was not so very long ago that Fairendale lost what remained of its loveliness, dear reader, but to its people, a whole lifetime has passed. They have forgotten what their beloved children used to sound like. They have forgotten the music of laughter. They have forgotten the pleasure of busy chatter. They have forgotten joy.

This once-grand kingdom has faded into a colorless shadow land, dark and sinister and cold.

The children were the light of the kingdom, you see. And now they are missing.

Why are they missing?

Well, now, that is a story worth telling.

# Secrets

At the time our story begins, the kingdom of Fairendale, though not as brilliant a land as it was before the days of its tyrant kings, overflows with color and music and the laughter and presence of children. Children peeking into a shop window, where the baker puts on his elaborate show of kneading bread on a wooden table and flipping it into the air and catching it with his eyes closed, pretending not to notice all of the eyes watching him. Children standing as near the shoemaker as they can manage, trying to predict how many times he will punch the awl through the leather before he decides the work is done. Children racing to the warm home of Arthur and Maude, where welcome lives in smiles.

Arthur is the village wood maker, a gentle man nearly as narrow as he is tall, with hair the color of dirt dusted with snow. Maude is his stringy wife, so thin and stretched she could very well disappear in the space between their red oak door and their home's front window, where she stands every morning to watch the village waking. One hardly sees her hair for the kerchief tied around it, but when wisps do escape their hiding place they are the color of wet sand. The two are terribly poor, but they are happy and generous, the kind of people who always have spice cookies to serve and a lesson to teach, especially when it comes to the friends of their two children, which is practically every child in the village. Arthur and Maude's children, Theo and Hazel, love everyone they meet. And everyone they meet loves them as well.

Arthur spends his days making ornate furniture in his workshop directly behind his family's humble cottage, though the villagers are much too poor to pay him a decent wage for his craftsmanship. Instead, they pay him in bread and shoes and milk. (He would have done it for nothing, but they insist. "You have growing children to feed, my good man," they say. As if they do not have children of their own.). When he is not working, Arthur teaches magic to his daughter and the village girls. He is quite proficient in the world of magic, having studied it for many years. Arthur does not have the gift of magic, of course. He, of anyone, understands quite how dangerous the gift of magic could be for a man or a boy who carries it. He merely teaches it, and the kingdom looks on with curiosity but no real alarm. Arthur is no threat. He is simply an old man with great knowledge. Great studied knowledge.

Magic, you see, is a very powerful gift in the kingdom of Fairendale and its surrounding lands. A male with magic is considered a grave danger to the royal line, for the king's crown can only be stolen by a magical male child. Females with magic are coveted, but, sadly, largely dismissed, mostly promised to princes in hopes that they will produce a magical child and secure the royal family's throne for many years to come. But they are never regarded as a serious threat of any kind. Of course we know how powerful females can be, but, alas, the land of our story is not so keen to notice such things.

Perhaps what is to come could be blamed on that very oversight.

The kingdom of Fairendale is ruled by King Willis, known as Your Most High King to the common people. He is not a very kind king, as we shall see in the pages to come. He is partly the reason Fairendale has lost its loveliness, though he is not entirely to blame. But we are getting ahead of ourselves.

King Willis was born the second son of King Sebastien, a poor boy from the kingdom of Lincastle, which one can find by traveling southeast to the very edge of the Violet Sea. Lincastle is not nearly so beautiful as Fairendale, and when King Sebastien was just a boy of sixteen, a magical boy of sixteen who believed he had been born on the wrong side of gentility, he decided to use his magic to steal Fairendale from the hands of its beloved Good King Brendon.

Every boy in the seven kingdoms of this magical land has been told the ancient stories all his life—stories where magic is more powerful than blood, where a boy born with magic can steal a throne right out of a royal line, where magic is a dangerous game of power and uncertainty and death. Every parent tells their sons the ancient stories in hopes that they will not try to overthrow a kingdom, as King Sebastien did, for a boy who tries this quest and fails it is banished, for all the rest of his days, to sail the Violet Sea, a sea full of monsters and the living dead and horrors one cannot even imagine.

King Sebastien, however, stole the crown and wore it for fifty-eight years before it passed to his son. He is an exception to the line of boys who have tried and failed.

It is not entirely easy for parents to convince their sons

that King Sebastien was an exception. It is, in fact, quite often that sons will interrupt the stories of their parents by saying, "But King Sebastien did it." So the stories these parents tell their sons become more dramatic, more fantastic, more dangerous every year, as I am sure you will understand. Parents who love their children do not want their boys banished forever on a sea as dangerous as a violet one.

Not that there are many boys who possess the gift of magic in the land of Fairendale.

No, there are not many at all.

There is only one.

In the cobblestone streets of Fairendale's village, magic is not hidden among the female children. And there are many female children with the gift of magic, presumably to provide the luxury of choice for a prince who wishes to marry a magical girl. So it is not entirely unusual to see shoes flying from one house to another or dolls walking beside a little girl instead of held in her arms or a wooden car, made from Arthur's scrap wood, piled beside his workshop, driving itself in and out of doorways.

Let us see what we have today: the daughter of a man who used to be a sailor, until he fell into the Violet Sea and was dragged to the bottom by mermaids; the daughter of Arthur and Maude, gathering scraps from Arthur's wood pile so they can make them fly; and her brother, dragging his best friend behind him.

"What if Papa needs those?" says Arthur's son, Theo. He is a handsome boy, with wild black curls and clear eyes the kind of blue that makes one wonder if the sky lost some pieces when he came into the world. His eyes dance with more merriment than concern, for Theo is a boy who loves fun as much as his sister does.

"Oh, Theo," his sister says, leaning against her gnarled staff. She has the same black curls, except they fall all the way down her back, rather than framing her face, which is home to the same blue eyes as her brother's. Hazel grins at Theo, her pink lips stretched wide across her teeth without showing them. She knows he is merely playing at concern. Arthur has never been cross with his children—not even when they were little and made it practically impossible to get any work done, what with Hazel's unrefined magic building boats in the air and Theo swiping perfectly good planks to duel with the other boys in the streets. The wood pieces always ended up splintering, but Arthur simply smiled and said he would find more. They did, after all, live near a populous wood.

Can you imagine a father like Arthur?

Yes, well, he is real. He is standing in the doorway of his cottage, watching his children with that same satisfied smile that has often passed his lips of late. Perhaps it is because his children are growing older. Perhaps it is because Hazel has advanced in her magic in such a way that has attracted the notice of the villagers. Perhaps for some other reason, such as only parents know.

"Come, Hazel," says the sailor's daughter. She is a girl of twelve, like Hazel, with milky white skin and flaming red hair and eyes the color of Fairendale's grassy fields. "Let us take these pieces into the streets. Entertain the younger children." She lifts her own staff, thicker than Hazel's, and a bit more crooked, though its hooked end is not nearly so curved as Hazel's, who uses hers to tend the village sheep.

"Make it fly first, Mercy," says the boy behind Theo. It might surprise you to know that this boy is the king's very own son.

Perhaps it is unusual to see a king's son with peasant children. But this particular king's son is a friendly child and an only child, and he has a kind mother. When Prince Virgil asked his mother if she might bring him some friends, Queen Clarion opened the palace doors and sent him along the dusty road to the village. He would find friends there, she said.

And he found three of them.

Theo was the first of the village boys to offer his toys to the lonely prince, instead of cringing away from him, afraid of offending the spoiled boy the village children had only heard about in stories. Prince Virgil is nothing like the stories. He loves Theo as if he were a brother. In fact, sometimes he wishes Theo were his brother, though Theo is a year younger than all the rest of them. A younger brother would suit Prince Virgil just fine.

Prince Virgil has a round, boyish face framed by tight curls the color of the village garden's soil just before the gardener waters it. His brown eyes, only a shade darker than his hair, smile for him when something amuses him—like magic, most days.

"You make it fly," Mercy says, her voice clipped and short. Mercy, you see, does not like Prince Virgil. She has a reason. Most females do.

"Too easy," Prince Virgil says. His dark eyes narrow, the fluffy brows drawn low. His fingers, wrapped around the smoothest staff of all those gathered here today, turn white. "I want to see if you can do it."

Mercy narrows her eyes and grips her wood chips tighter.

"You are afraid of the king?" she says, and her smile turns mocking. Years ago, when Hazel and Mercy urged him to use his gift of magic to make a wilting flower rise again, a simply rejuvenation spell, Prince Virgil told them that the king and queen forbade him to use his magic outside of the castle, away from his instructor. Prince Virgil glares at Mercy.

"Why do you bother bringing your staff at all?" Mercy says.

"Stop," Hazel says, and the wood chips suddenly suspend in the air. She looks from Mercy to Prince Virgil and back again. "It is really not so difficult," she says, and it is clear she is not talking about making wood chips fly.

We could fill in the blank for her, could we not, dear reader?

It is really not so difficult to get along.

It is really not so difficult to keep peace between friends.

It is really not so difficult to be kind.

It must be said, however, that Hazel will learn, soon enough, precisely how difficult it all is. But that will come.

For now, let us see what will happen when two girls and two boys take some wood scraps from a wood maker's pile and play with magic in the streets.

Hazel and Mercy skip ahead of Prince Virgil and Theo, their staffs clicking against the stone path. They laugh at the way the chips spin in the air, almost out of control, the magic keeping them afloat but not stopping their endless twisting in the invisible wind.

"Make something!" Theo says.

"What shall we make?" Hazel says, turning back to her brother.

Before he can answer, a few of the pieces move into position, becoming a wooden flower. Theo plucks it from the sky and leaps up six steps to hand it to a little girl watching him from the doorway of a home with scarlet flowers lining the walk. He pats her head and she grins up at him, awed that a boy like Theo would give notice at all to a girl of seven.

Hazel shakes her head at Theo, smiling, then points her staff at the pieces that remain, concentrating so hard she does not hear the call of "Dragon," that her brother flings in her direction. The wind whips her black hair around her face, her blue dress around her feet. She squints her eyes. Her friends watch her, knowing that something brilliant is coming. Hazel's eyes are always wide with wonder, except when she is performing magic.

Mercy, of course, could have made something absolutely spectacular by now, but she does not interfere. Sometimes the best way to be a friend is to permit a friend to struggle into doing something she may not have thought possible. And soon enough, the wood pieces rearrange themselves and become something quite brilliant indeed.

"A puppet!" Mercy says. "Well done!" She would not have thought of that. She had thought of a ship or a house or a castle, perhaps, something more impressive and intricately complicated. But a puppet is far more fun.

Hazel is always the best one for fun.

The children laugh at the puppet that is not really a puppet at all yet, because it is only wood.

"He needs a face!" Theo says. He raises his hand, and the puppet flies to him. He pulls a dagger from the belt tied around his tunic, where it sits beside the slips of parchment and charcoal piece he carries everywhere, and etches two eyes and a nose and a mouth.

He does not realize that the other children are staring at him. He does not see his sister's mouth hanging open. He does not notice his best friend take a step back. Just a small one. But enough.

"Now he is a real person?" he says, asking more than declaring. He holds up the wood with a carved face.

The children stare at him. He stares back, confused, until Prince Virgil says, "Did you just use magic to take the puppet from the sky?" The prince's eyes have turned nearly black, as if a storm lives inside them.

Prince Virgil knows all the stories, too. He knows that his throne can be stolen from his hands by a boy with magic. He knows he is assured nothing unless there is no boy in Fairendale who possesses this gift.

And it is unfortunate but true: He wants the throne, at least at this moment, more than he wants a friend. More than he wants a little brother.

It would be difficult to miss the stricken look that passes Theo's face, the way his skin pales just the slightest, the way his eyes turn the color of a sky at dawn rather than midday. Still he clears his throat. Still he says, "No." He looks at his sister.

"No," Hazel says, shaking her head. "He does not even have a staff." She looks at Mercy, then at Prince Virgil. "I knew what Theo wanted to do. I heard him and…" She waves her hand in the air. "Big sisters know their little brothers."

And who could not believe a sweet, innocent face like Hazel's? Because big sisters *do* know their little brothers, and of course she would realize what her brother wanted at nearly the same time he did, and of course she would use her magic so that he could make his contribution, an etched face on wood, to their magical fun. This boy who has no magic. This boy who is no danger. This boy who is her brother.

What she does not say, what she cannot ever say, is that she and Theo are twins, born the same day. Yes, she is the older sister, by seven whole minutes, but this would not help their case. Twins are rare and extraordinarily powerful, both born with a magic made stronger by the other's presence.

So if she told the truth, Mercy and Prince Virgil would know that, yes, her brother possesses the gift of magic, and it is a magic that does not need a staff, for it is far more powerful than any other gift.

Hazel widens her eyes more and arranges her face into as truthful a look as she can manage.

"It appeared that you used magic to grab it," Prince Virgil says. His eyes watch Theo, not Hazel. Fear is not as easy to hide when you are the one in danger. Theo's eyes tell the real truth, and he cannot change that. So he looks at the ground, not his friend.

"Oh, come, Prince Virgil," Hazel says. She touches the prince's arm, but he shakes her off. "He does not even have a staff." She looks at Mercy, as if pleading for help. "I put it into his hands. Believe me, I would know if my brother had magic." She takes the puppet from Theo and throws it up into the air, where it hangs suspended again. "You have a face," she says. "Now you need some hair."

Mercy plays along. She points her staff at some straw in the street, and it flaps to the puppet's head. She and Hazel spend the next few minutes searching for street scraps to clothe the puppet, trying not to notice the way the whole mood of their play darkens behind them. Soon enough they turn back to the two boys.

"Your turn, Prince Virgil," Hazel says. She is laughing again, and when Hazel laughs, it is nearly impossible not to laugh right along with her, which Theo and Mercy do.

Prince Virgil, however, is harder to break. He turns away. "I do not want to play anymore," he says, but he makes no move to leave.

"Come," Hazel says. She takes his arm, turns him back around. Mercy sends a burst of magic from her hands, and the puppet starts dancing on the air. The children watch, mesmerized by his twists and turns. It is a he, dressed to look like Arthur, dark brown boots strapped up to his knees, pants the color of the baker's bread, a sleeve-flapping shirt overlain with a tunic and tied with a bit of string.

Not one of them notices Prince Virgil's eyes turn mean and hard. Still he smiles and laughs and plays along.

Prince Virgil, you see, carries a secret of his own, a secret no man or woman or child must know. And that secret is clamping down on him right now, blackening his eyes and his vision and, yes, his heart.

Hazel flicks the wrist of the hand holding her staff and sends the puppet flipping, one turn after another. The children laugh again at the awkward piece of wood bending and turning and now walking and running, as if it is a miniature version of their long-legged father.

"Make him talk, Prince Virgil!" Hazel says.

Prince Virgil gives a violent shake of his head.

"Please!" Hazel says. "Do not be a prude."

"I am no prude," Prince Virgil says. "I just do not want to play. I must return to the castle now."

Mercy flicks her wrist, and the puppet's mouth opens. "Whatever is the matter, Prince Virgil? Lost your magic?" it says.

It takes only a second for Prince Virgil's hand to reach out and grab the puppet and hurl him to the ground, where he breaks into a thousand wood scrap pieces. Prince Virgil's friends look at him, their eyes wide. Never before have they seen something like this from their friend Prince

Virgil.

He stares back at them, ashamed at this thing he has done, this thing that has, by the looks of it, shocked and perhaps even frightened his only friends in the world. But he is more ashamed of what he cannot do.

"Magic is foolish," Prince Virgil says in a voice as cold as his eyes, and then he turns away, gripping his staff tighter than ever.

The children watch him until he disappears.

It is nearly dark. Hazel and Theo sit outside the doors of their home. The cottages of the kingdom do not have porches, only a small patch of earth lined by flowers on either side. This is where the villagers gather at the end of their days, for if there is one thing of superior beauty over all the others in this fair land, it is the last lights of the evening sky. Just as the sun touches the shining gray stone of Fairendale castle's West tower, it lights the Violet Sea tributary and the whole sky on fire, such as a painting of brilliant colors could never capture. One can only stare. It is a spectacular sight, those oranges and reds and purples both above and below the bridge Prince Virgil crosses every day to see his friends. If one is very fortunate and does not need to blink at the exact moment the sun disappears beneath the land, one will see a ring of water swallow a mermaid's tail. Those who see it are rumored to have good fortune for all the rest of their days.

The villagers of Fairendale have never seen a mermaid's tale at that exact moment, for mermaids are sly creatures who do not grant their good fortune to just anyone. The people remain collected on their elaborate lawns until the sun disappears and the sky darkens and all the stars line up in their majestic places. They stare at those stars and breathe their day's end, and then they return to their homes for the night's preparations before retiring to sleep. It is the same ritual every night of their lives, yet it never grows old.

Tonight, Hazel and Theo sit a bit removed from their parents, which is not so unusual for children of their age. They do not always want to be where their parents are, but they certainly do not want to miss the night's soft arrival. Tonight they are talking in whispers, sorting through what happened earlier today in the streets, for they have not had a safe moment until now, the time when their father and mother talk with one another.

"Why do you remain friends with Prince Virgil?" Hazel

says. "He is a horrid boy."

"He is lonely," Theo says. "He is a prince, from a different world than ours. He is not easy to understand. I suspect we are not, either."

"All the more reason he should not be here," Hazel says. It is unusual to hear her talk so harshly as this. You will remember that Hazel is mostly fun and games and good nature, but today's events have shaken her badly. Fear has a way of turning a heart in quite a new direction sometimes, hardening it in protection, rather than softening it in love.

Theo, however, still loves his friend. "He does not have any friends at the castle," he says. Theo does not look at his sister but stares instead at the sky. He does not really want to have this argument. Perhaps he should have pulled his chair closer to his mother's.

"But he is horrid," Hazel says. "He does not wish to ever have fun."

Now Theo looks at his sister. His eyebrows pull close to his eyes. "You would never tell me to let anyone else play alone."

Hazel looks toward the tributary, where she has always hoped she would see a mermaid. Just one glimpse. Just one tail. Just one promise for good fortune all the rest of her days. "I do not like him," she says.

Her brother does not answer, and even in the fading dark one can see Hazel's eyes soften. Her brother has been her dearest friend since she was born. "I do not know what it is about him, Theo," she says. "But there is something that frightens me. It is as if he carries a dark secret. I have seen it, in his eyes, though I do not know what it is."

"I carry a secret," Theo says. "So he is like me." His eyes rest on Hazel's face. "He is like us."

"Yes, I suppose he is," Hazel says. "But I fear he may be more dangerous than we want to believe."

"That is foolish," Theo says. "Prince Virgil is our friend. He would never hurt us. He loves us, as we love him."

Oh, reader. If only being a friend were an accurate measure for good and evil. If only we could know for sure that friends could never hurt us simply because they love us. But we know that is not true. And poor Theo. He will know soon enough.

"You used magic," Hazel says. "He knows."

Theo hisses, an effort to quiet her. He glances at his parents, still talking. They do not seem to notice anything but each other and the fiery sky. Theo sighs. If his parents heard of his mistake, they would never permit him to play with Prince Virgil again. They would never permit him to sit in the back of his cottage kitchen, pretending to work on whittling but listening to Arthur teach magic to the village girls. They would never permit him to be anything but a boy, and he is more than a boy. So much more.

"I know," Theo says. His shoulders sag. "I did not intend to do it."

"You cannot make foolish mistakes," Hazel says. "Not around a horrid boy like Prince Virgil."

"Please stop calling him horrid," Theo says, his voice jagged and prickly. He loves his friend. But he also loves his sister.

"He is the most dangerous of all the village boys," Hazel says. "You must be more careful."

"Yes," Theo says. "I must." He must. "I will not let it happen again."

"Especially not around Prince Virgil," Hazel says, as if she truly wants her brother to understand her urgency, as if he has not already fully understood it, as if, perhaps, he has not comprehended the gravity of such a mistake.

"Yes," he says again, his whisper just a touch sharper than it had been before. Then, thinking better of his bother, he says, "Thank you for stepping in today."

"Do you think they believed us?" Hazel says.

"Certainly they did," Theo says, though he is anything but certain, truth be told. Hazel is a reliable source, which makes her not a great liar. He is not certain at all if their story was believed by anyone who saw his mistake.

Theo and Hazel smile at one another and then turn their eyes to the fading sky and its orange sun, which hangs in a sliver above the fresh-water cove ending the Violet Sea's reach onto the village grounds. Now is just the moment when the stories say one might see the elusive mermaid's tale. Theo stares, afraid to blink, until his eyes begin to water, until they burn like the sun did mere moments ago. And all his effort is rewarded, dear reader. Just before his eyelids close, he sees the tail and hears its subsequent splash.

He does not say anything to his sister, who blinked at the exact wrong time.

He keeps this secret to himself.

Across the Violet Sea tributary and the curved gray stone bridge, where flowers burst even through the gaps of rock, Prince Virgil sits all alone, watching the sky long after it has turned dark and the stars come out in earnest. His staff leans against a corner in his room, useless to him. A staff only does what a magician bids it, and Prince Virgil is no magician.

He has only been thinking about what he did earlier today. Only been feeling bad. Only been wrestling with questions and going over and over the events to imagine they had played out any other way.

Magic is foolish? What kind of prince who is supposed to have the gift of magic, who is supposed to be a king in a magical kingdom like Fairendale, says such foolish words? They will surely guess his secret now. What will he do now?

"We will protect the throne," his father had said the day Prince Virgil tried to do magic like his mother and failed. "We will pretend. No one will have to know. A king does not use his magic, at any rate." King Willis had sent for all the prophets in the land, from as far away as Guardia, the kingdom in the far, far north that was said to never know warmth, only ice and cold, hoping to discover what was wrong with his son. Queen Clarion's magic, coupled with his, should have been strong enough to produce a magical son. Why had Prince Virgil been born with no magic?

The prophets all said the same thing. Only the worthy are given magic.

Only the worthy.

His mother had cried. His father had raged. The prophets had looked sadly on, and then the king, flying into the same fit of rage he always did when the prophets pronounced their diagnosis, which was nothing new to anyone in the royal family, threw the prophets into the dungeon for their efforts. After the prophets had left his presence, Prince Virgil, every time, would watch the king pace the throne room, pontificating on the injustice of magic and how a royal line should be secured by blood rather than a silly gift, appearing to forget altogether that magic was how His Most High King had gained the throne in the first place. King Willis would talk until his wife quietly reminded him that if they wanted to keep this knowledge a secret from the kingdom, they must silence their monologues. By "they," of course, the queen meant King Willis. She was a woman of few words, where her husband was a man of many.

"What kind of king is born without magic?" King Willis whispered when the one hundred forty-second prophet—a bent, white-haired old man—came to tell them what they had already heard from so many before. King Willis entertained them all, after the first several, only because he hoped that someone would bear different, better news—that his son did, in fact, have magic. It had merely taken a number of years to show itself. But, alas, there was no cure for "born without the gift of magic," and King Willis, to preserve his own skin and that of his son, threw them all into the dungeon beneath the dungeons, a place no man would willingly go. No man, that is, except the trusty assistant cook Calvin, who is sent every morning at 7 o'clock and again at 6 o'clock in the evening to deliver bread and water to the prisoners. The prisoners have learned to ration their nourishment in the hours between.

Fairendale and the lands beyond hold no more prophets now. They all live in the darkest place one can imagine, a place where eyes grow accustomed to seeing nothing. And, sadly, their hearts have grown accustomed to waving away hope, for there is none to be found for a man in the dungeon below the dungeons. No one but Calvin and the royal family, and, perhaps, the captain of the king's guard, even know they exist.

Why does the king keep them? Why does he not kill them? Well, now, our king is not so heartless as that. He does not want the blood of one hundred forty-two prophets on his hands. There are stories, of course, stories about what happens to a man who might kill a prophet. Our king does not wish to discover for himself whether those stories are indeed true. So he gives his prisoners water and feeds them, twice a day. And they live. Though we might all agree they do not really live at all.

Prince Virgil thinks of them sometimes, trapped in the same cell, pressed against each other in the cold, unable to see one face from another. He has never been to the dungeons below the dungeons, but he imagines it a frightful place, as any place too far for light to reach it would very well be.

"Virgil," Queen Clarion says. He turns to the doorway, where she stands in shadows. Her eyes look black from here, though he knows them to be the deepest blue of the evening sky. "What are you doing out here?"

"Watching the sunset, Mother," he says.

She laughs. "The sunset finished hours ago, dear." Queen Clarion steps out onto the stone balcony, her hand searching for her son's shoulder. It is dark on his private terrace, for he has so lost himself in his thoughts that he has forgotten to light the torches.

Her hand warms his skin. His mother always feels warm to him, perhaps from all the kindness that lives inside her. She is the kindest woman Prince Virgil has ever known, outside of Maude, who is much older and much less beautiful than his mother.

Queen Clarion visits her son's chambers every night to bid him goodnight. Though most queens leave their children to others, Queen Clarion has always loved her boy with a fierce love that does not depend on whether or not he carries the gift of magic. She does not care that she gave up her great gift, as every magical parent must, so that he could get nothing. He is her son. That is the only story a mother's love tells.

She touches Prince Virgil's curls. He tilts his head onto her shoulder, which he almost never does anymore. He is a boy of twelve, after all. The unexpected gesture makes his mother drop a kiss to the top of his head.

And that is what makes Prince Virgil feel safe enough to question, to work out his bothers, to lay them at the feet of one who loves him with a love that might very well listen. This question has been torturing him all night, stinging him as the wind that gusts from the north never could. "Are you disappointed you gave up your gift of magic for me?" he says.

If one could see her lovely face in all the shadows, Queen Clarion would not look the least bit surprised. She is a good mother. She has already guessed what has kept her boy out on his balcony long into the evening. She knows he has spent his day with magical children in the village. She knows he does not understand the reasons for a boy born without magic. She knows that he wishes he could have this gift, more than he has ever wished another thing in all the world.

"No," she says. "I am not disappointed in the slightest." Her voice is sure and solid and strong. He breathes the relief it brings.

And then he says, "Why was I born without magic?"

She does not answer immediately. Her eyes fix on the dark sky, a painting of tiny pinpoints of light. But Prince Virgil notices, because he is looking, that she is no longer smiling. "We do not know why," she says, but there is something that happens when Queen Clarion lies. At least Prince Virgil suspects it happens when she is lying, for he has only seen it once before, when he asked about his Uncle Wendell and why he was banished from the kingdom of Fairendale, and his mother answered simply, "He was not a wise man." The lids of his mother's eyes get the slightest bit thicker, her lips the slightest bit thinner. It would take an observant child to notice such small details. Prince Virgil has always been one of those.

"But you and Father had magic," he says. "Why do I not?"

"Well," his mother says. "Well."

They are quiet for some moments. Prince Virgil wonders if she is ever going to answer, and then Queen Clarion turns to her son and takes both his hands in hers. "I think it is time we talked with your father," she says. She drops his hands and moves gracefully, as she always does, back into the deeper shadows just outside Prince Virgil's balcony door, where a woman like Queen Clarion is prone to standing. It is not right, reader, of course it is not, but in Fairendale, the virtues that Queen Clarion carries deep inside—gentleness and kindness and love—are not the virtues that are said to be the right ones, the ones that can rule a kingdom well. The powerful virtues in this upside-down kingdom—ruthlessness, selfishness, perfidy—those are the characteristics that give a kingdom to a man like King Willis.

A woman like Queen Clarion cannot do much here. At least not yet.

But let us follow Queen Clarion and her son into the shadows and through the doorway and down the long, torchlit hallway with ceilings high enough to comfortably accommodate three giants standing atop the shoulders of one another. Let us enter the royal chamber, where our great king awaits.

The king, of course, is not waiting for his son or his wife. He is not a man accustomed to spending much time with the lesser people, which is precisely how he views his son and his wife. Lesser, for they are not important rulers of a kingdom. Lesser, for one is a woman and one a child. Lesser, for they are not him.

King Willis is a man who keeps himself busy running a kingdom, though the kingdom is mostly peaceful, and a man running a kingdom can hardly be counted upon to sup with his wife and only son, much less converse with them in the margins between settling disputes (there are none) and making kingdom decisions (what kind of sweet rolls he would like today) and protecting his people from the dangers of the outside world (no one has invaded the land since his father stole the throne).

Yes, reader, it really is a tragedy of the most avoidable kind. A child is a transformative gift. A father should always want to know his child.

The king, even now, is waiting on someone else and has no thought reserve in his large brain to waste on his wife and son. He does not wonder what they are doing. He does not consider leaving the throne room to bid his son goodnight. If one were to look inside his mind for just a moment, one would see that he is not in this room at all, but very far away, waiting.

He waits for someone very like the other one hundred forty-two people hidden in the deepest bowels of the castle, where one can easily forget them if one were a man such as King Willis. A woman is coming, after all these years. A woman he hopes will bear good news where all the others brought bad.

So when the queen knocks on the door at the precise time he expects another, King Willis, of course, believes it is the one on whom he waits. It does not even cross his mind that his son and wife might stand on the other side of the door, about to enter and soil his perfectly planned evening with unexpected questions and wonderings. He does not expect that he will be sharing any secrets this evening.

But, alas, doors do not always open on what we expect.

The king calls out in a jovial voice, a voice very unlike the one Queen Clarion and Prince Virgil have heard before today, though not often. "Come in, come in, please," the king says.

The royal chamber is a large room of red and gold. It

is the largest room you can imagine, with such a distance from the door to the throne that one cannot even see the face of the royal body sitting on the throne, even if one has perfect vision. One would have to walk halfway down the red velvet carpet to see clearly enough to know whether a king was happy or angry that one had interrupted whatever it is a king does in such a room as this one. Its ceilings are as high as the hallway ones, but these are carved with elaborate works of art, pictures of nighttime skies, a portrait of the giant who guards the Great Mountains, the faces of past kings who do not share the same family but all share the same gift: magic.

King Willis is surprised enough by the ones who enter that a "You" escapes his lips and booms all the way down the carpet to his wife and son. They stop for a moment, familiar with the contempt that meets them. And then he says, "Come," so they continue on. By the time they are halfway down the carpet, the king's face is blank, as if he is not made of emotion at all, as if he is merely a body on a throne. Prince Virgil tries to keep his eyes on the red drapes hanging from a gold tunnel attached to the ceiling. He tries not to look at his father, even from the corners of his eyes; his father is an intimidating man, large in body and spirit and voice. Jewels blink at Prince Virgil from the throne as he moves closer, shimmering in the light from candles on gold pillars that line the walk from entrance to throne.

Garth, the king's manservant, stands at the foot of the throne, at the bottom of the steps, ready to fetch a drink or some food or to simply help the king rise from his seat, since it has become difficult for His Most High King to squeeze in and out of it without a little extra help. His body, fed by the abundance of wealth and plenty, spills over the golden arm rests, a stark contrast to the servants in the room, who grow gaunt in their lack. It is the very picture King Willis prefers: a physical proof of the difference between wealthy and poor.

"Well?" King Willis says when his wife and son have reached the place just in front of Garth and done their obligatory curtsy and bow. "What is it, now?" He looks toward the door, as if he is already wishing them away.

Imagine facing a man like that with nothing to offer but questions.

But Queen Clarion, for all her kindness, also possesses another virtuous characteristic: bravery.

Bravery is what takes her foot and plants it on the first step and then the second, and one after another. Bravery is what reaches her hand toward her son to pull him forward with her. Bravery is what brings her to the space that is inches in front of the king, where almost no one goes, and it is what bows her head low, and it is also what pulls these words from her lips:

"Virgil has been asking questions."

"Virgil has been asking questions," King Willis repeats. He looks at his son, as if surprised that he is there. "Well, my queen, Virgil is a child. Children ask question, do they not?" He looks at his wife as if she is simply another commoner interrupting his noonday meal. They stare at one another for a time. And then King Willis seems to recognize something in Queen Clarion's eyes, for he says, "What sorts of questions has Virgil been asking?" though it is clear that he is not at all interested in the answer.

Queen Clarion nudges her son forward and nods at him in that way a mother has, encouraging him to find his bravery and speak with a king. She squeezes his hand in her own. A gentle touch. An empowering touch. A touch that says, "I am here."

Prince Virgil has only spoken to his father three times in his life—once when he was merely a baby and Queen Clarion brought him into the royal chamber to show King Willis that his son had learned to say Father, once when he was a young boy of five and Queen Clarion brought him into the royal chamber so he could explain to King Willis why the curtains in the ballroom were missing three inches from their bottom (he did it, reader, because no one ever opened the curtains, and there were so many windows, so much light, and the room had the best view in the whole castle. He merely wanted to see outside. He did the best thing he thought possible), and another time when the king and queen discovered, after the first ninety-nine prophets said the same old thing—that Prince Virgil was, surely and certainly, a boy born without the gift of magic.

And now, today. Only four times in his twelve years has Prince Virgil spoken to his father.

He stammers a little. (Wouldn't you, dear reader? If you were speaking to a king, a king who rules a whole land, a king you did not really know, a king who is your father? Of course.)

"W-w-why was I b-b-born without m-m-magic?" Prince Virgil says. He hates the way his voice sounds so squeaky and nervous and weak. He would like to have a different voice, one more like Theo's, who sounds like a boy but also sounds like he may be on his way to becoming a man. He does not want to disappoint his father with this voice. So he does not say more.

His father looks at him. Queen Clarion squeezes Prince Virgil's hand, and that is the only reason Prince Virgil looks at his father. And when his father does not answer, Prince Virgil clears his throat and tries again, encouraged by his mother's warmth. This time his voice sounds thicker, though not any older. "Why, Father?" he says.

The king lets loose a great laugh, which shakes his whole belly in a way that looks much like waves rolling across an ocean, pitching into a shore. Prince Virgil tries to keep his eyes on the king's face rather than that great grey velvet ocean with buttons that hardly fasten anymore. A gold piece at the center of his father's belly is held on by a tight belt that looks as if it may burst at any moment. Prince Virgil lifts his eyes up, away from the shaking. The crown on the king's head is large and shiny, with red and blue and purple jewels studded in all its spikes. It is so heavy, and King Willis has so much extra flesh on his forehead, that the wearing of it produces an almost permanent scowl, even when he is laughing. Prince Virgil feels the urge to laugh at the frightful sight.

"Son," the king says. "Of course you were born with magic." The king glances at his manservant, Garth, as if Garth has not listened at doorways and heard what one hundred forty-two prophets have told the royal family in years past.

"No," Prince Virgil says. He looks at his mother, who

lets out a breath. "No, Father, I was not."

"Silence!" King Willis roars. The whole royal chamber echoes the word, and the world holds still, everyone too frightened to even breathe. "Leave us," King Willis says, a touch softer. The king does not specify to whom he speaks, but Garth has already begun to move.

Queen Clarion smiles at the meek, homely boy. "Thank you, Garth," she says. King Willis does not know his manservant's name, for this is not something important to his life and well being. But Queen Clarion knows the names of every servant in the house.

"Yes, m'lady," Garth says, his eyes on the floor.

King Willis moves in a flash, surprising for his bulk. Prince Virgil hears the smack and sees his mother's face twist to the side. Did King Willis hit her? Did he strike Queen Clarion on the cheek? What kind of man would do something so cruel and unnecessary?

Well, reader, men do cruel and unnecessary things for all kinds of reasons. Arrogance. Conviction. Fear. For our king, it is some of all of those that move his hand.

Queen Clarion touches her cheek, staring at the floor. "How dare you!" roars the king. "How dare you address my manservant by name!" His hands fly, his arms bouncing against his sides and then spreading back out again. "They are little more than dogs. They do not deserve a name."

Prince Virgil stares at his father. This explosion does not surprise Queen Clarion, but it surprises Prince Virgil, indeed. He has never seen his father this angry, over something so simple as calling a boy by his proper name. Prince Virgil looks at Garth, this boy who is older than him by four years? Five? Perhaps more? It is hard to tell on a face like his. Garth pulls at his brown belt splitting his deep green tunic in half, as if unsure of what he should do.

"Go!" King Willis roars again.

Garth scurries toward the door, like one of the mice Prince Virgil frees from the traps in the castle library. He does not mind the mice so much. A few of them are blind and merely enjoy sitting in a place filled with the scent of ancient days. Or so he believes. He does not know, of course. Mice cannot talk.

As soon as Garth has closed the door behind him, King Willis takes a deep breath. One. Two. Three. Then he clears his throat. From the sweat collecting on his brow, one might think the king was uncomfortable or nervous or caught.

Yes. Perhaps he is caught.

"Why do you not have magic?" King Willis says. "That is a question your mother can answer just as well as I can."

King Willis glares at his wife, as if she is to blame for putting him in this uncomfortable circumstance.

"No," Queen Clarion says. Her voice is kind, but the words hold a steel bar. Prince Virgil watches it take a swing at his father's face. But Queen Clarion is not yet done. "This is a question for his father." She peers at the king. Prince Virgil stares at the red flower on her cheek, an exaggerated hand.

Were he to look at his father's hands at that very moment, he would see the king's fingers clenching into fists, turning the knuckles white. One might, perhaps, suppose that King Willis would strike Queen Clarion again, but our king has more discretion than this. Discretion, of course, can be lost in a moment of fury, as it was mere moments ago, but King Willis, for now, is calm.

Prince Virgil peels his eyes from his mother's damaged cheek and turns them on his father. His anger bites out words. "I want to hear it from you," he says.

King Willis waves a hand. "You have magic," he says. "Dormant magic. We have not found the right prophets to uncover it yet."

"There are no more prophets," Prince Virgil says.

"Ah," the king says. His eyes turn glittery. "That is where you are wrong, my boy. There is one who comes this very night."

Prince Virgil tilts his head. Could this prophet, perhaps, carry the answers to questions he has wondered all his life? "Who?" he says to his father.

King Willis leans forward in his chair. "A prophetess," the king says. "Come to bring good news, I suspect."

Prince Virgil shakes his head. He has hoped for so long, through one hundred forty-two of them. Is there any hope left? And if there were, should he waste it on something as uncertain as this?

"Tell him," Queen Clarion says, and Prince Virgil looks at his mother's face. Her eyes are icy and hard and unsafe. So he moves his gaze to his father.

"Tell me what?" Prince Virgil says. He keeps his eyes on King Willis, who glares at the queen.

"Ask your father what he ever did of magic before you were born," Queen Clarion says. Her voice is marble, cold and unbreakable.

Prince Virgil does not know if he wants to hear the answer to this question. But he asks it anyway. "Did you practice magic before I was born?"

King Willis stares at him for far too many moments. He does not think his father will answer. And then King Willis surprises them all. His face softens.

“Come closer,” the king says. He folds himself back into the throne, and the gold lets out a squeal of protest. Prince Virgil steps to his side. Queen Clarion sits on the stairs and smooths her billowing blue skirt so it fans out across the red carpet. King Willis takes a deep breath. “In the kingdom of Fairendale,” his father begins, “magic rules the throne.”

Yes. Prince Virgil knows this.

“Eighty-three years ago,” King Willis says, “my father stole the throne from a man who had only the smallest threads of magic. A girl to carry his name.” He looks at Prince Virgil with shadowed eyes. “Your grandfather had some of the most powerful magic in all the lands. And so he took the throne from the king who had so little. He was about your age, I think. How old are you, son?”

“Twelve,” Prince Virgil says, trying to imagine leading a rebellion at his age.

“Well, then,” King Willis says. “Never mind. Father was sixteen.” The king clears his throat. “For years my father ruled the throne with justice and set the people in their rightful place. You must understand that in the days of King Brendon, the common people ate a great feast on the lawn of the castle every Year’s Last Day. They would visit the castle. They would walk its halls and eat its leftover food and take whatever it was they needed." His eyes narrow, just the slightest bit. "That is not a proper way to run a kingdom, you see."

King Willis glares at his wife, then looks back at his son. "So my father restored the balance that every kingdom needs. The common people remained in the village. The royal line remained in the castle. Still, to this day. It is as it should be." He stares at his son, as if trying to determine whether Prince Virgil feels the same. But all Prince Virgil can think about is his best friend being a commoner. What would it be like to sup with his friend? What would it be like to play hide-and-seek in those great halls? What would it be like to swim out in the cove, protecting one another from the mermaids?

"Your grandfather was forty-four years old when he brought me into the world," King Willis says. "But there are rules to magic."

Prince Virgil does not know any of the rules of magic, for he has never had a reason to learn them. He does not know about vanishing spells or precisely how magic is passed on to children or that something cannot be magically created from nothing, for no one has ever formally trained him, since he did not have the gift.

"When a magic person has a child, all of his magic

passes to that child," King Willis says. "His son or daughter receives the gift of magic." King Willis looks at the floor. Prince Virgil wonders, more now than ever, why the magic did not pass to him, then. If magic passes from parents to children, why was he skipped?

"There's a catch," Queen Clarion says. She looks at her husband.

"Yes, a catch," King Willis says. His fingers turn white against the throne now. "If there are any other children, they do not get a single ounce of magic. Not one single ounce." King Willis stares out toward the door, as if he is seeing something entirely different than this room and these people and the candles painting shapes onto the wall.

Prince Virgil still does not understand. But he knows better than to ask any questions. He looks at his mother. She stares at the king, waiting for what comes next.

King Willis rearranges himself in his chair. "I have a brother," he says. "An older brother."

The words slam against Prince Virgil's throat. An older brother? But the only brother his father had was Wendell, a younger brother who was banished from Fairendale long before Prince Virgil was born. Because he was not a wise man.

And then another thought scratches past all the others.

If his uncle got all the magic and his father got none, where was the hope for him?

"But," Prince Virgil says. "But where is he?"

"Banished," King Willis says, and for a moment his eyes look just the tiniest bit sad. Could he have loved his brother, reader? Could he have adored him in the way younger brothers often adore older brothers? Could he have grieved when his brother left?

"For kindness," Queen Clarion says, her voice almost a whisper.

But the words, unfortunately, are not lost on her husband. He tries to stand again, but this time he has slumped too far and cannot rise without taking the golden chair with him. And, alas, its weight is greater even than his own, and it pulls him back down. "For treason," he says, and the sadness is gone. There is only anger now.

"What was his name?" Prince Virgil says.

"Wendell," King Willis says.

Prince Virgil shakes his head. "But you told me he was younger," he says.

"To protect you," King Willis says. "To protect the whole kingdom."

Prince Virgil tries not to think what this may mean. "What did he do?" he says instead.

"That matters not," King Willis says. "What matters is that the throne passed to me. And I had no magic." He lets out a great, long breath. Prince Virgil is close enough to smell the rye bread and garlic. Prince Virgil loves rye bread, especially when dipped in Cook's best chicken soup. King Willis, for his part, prefers sweet rolls. But regardless of what he prefers, it has been hours now since the king has had something to eat. In fact, his stomach is rumbling at this very moment, reminding him that it is long past his normal dining hour, because he has been waiting on someone. Waiting on someone who, every minute, is another minute late to the agreed-upon meeting at the agreed-upon time. King Willis does not like when people are late. King Willis is a punctual man himself, particularly when it comes to food.

Minute by minute, he is growing hungrier. And more peevish.

"Where is my uncle now?" Prince Virgil says.

"No one knows," Queen Clarion says, at the same time King Willis says, "Dead." The king and queen stare at one another, neither one willing to back down from their answers.

"Your uncle," Queen Clarion begins. Now that she knows her husband will not be rising from his chair without help, she will tell her son the truth. "He had a kind heart. He could not bear to see people go hungry or sleep cold. So he used his magic to give them bread and blankets and houses that kept them dry in the spring rains."

"A king is not a wish-giver!" King Willis roars. "That is not the point of magic! A king is a ruler!" And, dear reader, should we be able to go back in time, we would see just how much our king sounds like his father before him, the day his brother, Wendell, was banished from the kingdom. They really are two of a kind.

King Willis lets out another breath. Prince Virgil turns away this time, afraid he will be sick. "We had beggars, lined up for miles. My brother wanted to help them all." The king's face is red and splotchy. "It was just like the days of that weak King Brendon. We could not have that kind of kingdom again, you see? My father cleaned it up. We could not be wish givers or we would never be permitted to rule. The people would run wild, as they did in those days. It would be uncivilized. They would take liberties and sleep on the steps of the castle and break into our halls and dirty up our floors. They would expect handouts when they were fully capable of working for themselves."

"A king should help his people," says Queen Clarion. She has risen from her seat. Her face is red, too, but it is her heart that has our attention. Her heart, you see, is so tender. So sad. So broken.

What no one in the room has said is that Queen Clarion was chosen to rule the kingdom alongside Prince Wendell, when he became king. She was brought to Fairendale castle as a child of six, as the promised bride of Prince Wendell upon reaching the age of sixteen. But when Prince Wendell was sent away in disgrace, she was forced to marry his brother, Prince Willis, instead.

Her misery is great, as I am sure you can imagine. We must not let her beauty and kind countenance fool us. Queen Clarion loved her betrothed desperately, and when he disappeared, he took a large part of her heart with him. She tried her best to love King Willis, but he was the opposite of her beloved in every way.

It is not easy to love a man so disappointing.

"A king should rule his people," King Willis says. "A king should make them work. A king should be a leader, not a magician who grants all their wishes and makes their lives easy. Workers get lazy when they have no work."

Prince Virgil does not argue with King Willis, but if he were a different boy, a braver boy, perhaps, he would side with his mother. He has seen the poor in their homes, after all. He has seen the way they work, the way they play, the way their stomachs are almost never full because there is almost never enough. He once tried to give his friends scraps from his own rich feasts, but as soon as he opened his pack and took out the first chunk of bread, his nurse slapped his hand hard enough to make it bleed and looked around the village, as if fearing for her life. Then she poured the contents of the sack down the well where the villagers drew their water. He watched the villagers watching his nurse, stricken. And then Arthur climbed down inside the well and picked out all the soggy food so it would not contaminate their water supply. He never tried to bring food to the villagers again.

Prince Virgil decides to steer the discussion in a safer direction, so his father does not guess what he is thinking. King Willis is staring at him, and he does not want to be the disappointing son. So he says, "But you had magic." And this time he looks at his mother.

Her eyes glisten. "Yes," she says. "I did have magic."

"Your mother had the most powerful magic in the kingdom of Fairendale when she was young," King Willis says, the first good word he has spoken of his wife in a very long time. "That is why she was chosen as a queen." He looks at his son again, stroking his chin. "We thought her power would be strong enough to pass along to you, even without my contribution."

"But it was not," Prince Virgil says.

"We suspect it is because it takes two magical parents to make a magical child," Queen Clarion says. "Though we do not know for sure."

"So I must keep this a secret," Prince Virgil says.

"Yes," King Willis says.

"But how did the people not know about my uncle?" Prince Virgil says.

"The kingdom believes we are twins," King Willis says. "My father had the foresight to spread this story early enough. No one thought to question it. As far as the people are concerned, I had the gift of magic before it passed along to you."

"But someone will surely find out, Father. Will they not?" Prince Virgil says.

His father's eyes grow dark, a muddy pit in a candlelit room. King Willis leans forward again, as though reaching for Prince Virgil without extending his arms. "No," he says. His voice is not loud this time, which makes it all the worse. "No. They will never find out. The throne will never pass from our hands."

"But they will surely know," Prince Virgil says. "When I cannot perform magic."

“We will make the necessary arrangements. There may yet be another way. A magic way,” King Willis says, and Prince Virgil is wondering what that might possibly mean when another knock echoes into the great room.

“Ah,” King Willis says. “Ah, yes. Forty minutes late. It is about time.” He settles back into his seat.

# Plans

Sebastien was born a very poor boy in the kingdom of Lincastle. A nothing. A no one. Except that he had magic.

And this would mean everything.

Every night before bed, his father told him stories of the great kingdom of Fairendale, the most beautiful of all the kingdoms, ruled by a family with magic. They were only stories to him, until one day the town prophet, a man called Iddo, told him another story, about men who had stolen thrones in the most beautiful land because of their magic.

"But only royal blood sits on a throne," Sebastien said. Even at eight, he was a sharp boy. He knew the rules of the lands.

"Oh, no," Iddo said. His eyes flashed. "Only a magic boy sits the throne of Fairendale."

"But princes are always born with magic," Sebastien said.

"No," the prophet said. "Not always. Some are not. Some are not princes but princesses. Some thrones are stolen." And then he looked at Sebastien as if he knew what was to come.

Perhaps he did. He was a prophet, after all.

Sebastien walked home that night with shaking legs. He had magic. His father also had magic once, before he passed the gift to Sebastien. He had heard about his father's magic, how he was revered as one of the most skilled in all of Lincastle. Why had his father not tried to steal a kingdom with his great power? His father could have been a ruler. Sebastien could have been born a prince. They could have lived in a large palace with gleaming stone walls and beds that were not lumpy and fires that never went out, instead of the cold cottage that never had enough space to promise restful sleep the nights his mother cried out in pain.

So he asked his father one night, sitting by the fire that would not burn through dawn, wiping the sweat from his mother's brow as she tossed and turned on a pallet of sticky straw. Why had he never stolen a throne? Why had he not tried to better their lives? Why had he stayed here, poor, dismissed, suffering?

"There are more important things than ruling a kingdom," his father said.

That was the first time Sebastien realized that they did not believe the same things, he and his father. For you see, there was nothing more important than ruling a throne.

Then his mother died on a starless night, and Sebastien wept silently in a great chasm of grief while he watched his father bury her body. That night a new question began to take shape: Would his mother have died if she had been a queen, with access to medicine and food and warmth?

Without his mother to care for, Sebastien's father began to teach him magic. Sebastien admired his father for his great knowledge, but he soon exceeded even his father's skill. "You will do great good with your gift," his father said, after every lesson.

And Sebastien would nod and close himself in his room, where the question he had asked his father would haunt him even after he closed his eyes. Waking or sleeping, he could not escape it. Why had his father never stolen a throne?

It did not take long before the question became a questioning of himself. Why did he not steal a throne?

His father began to suspect what hid in Sebastien's

heart. One day he pulled his son aside and said, "A man should not go where he is not welcome. You cannot do this, my son. You cannot steal a kingdom. Your mother and I are peaceful people." His eyes held depths of sadness that even Sebastien could not bear.

Still, Sebastien merely shook him off. His mother would be alive if it were not for his father's peace. And he was nothing like his father. Oh, no. In Sebastien the need for power and wealth and vengeance grew and grew and grew until it had nearly taken over the entirety of his heart like a black ink blot subjected to water. He began to study the dark magic, beneath the eyes of Iddo. There was nothing his father could do to stop it.

"Never use your magic for ill," Sebastien's father told him another day. "Dark magic demands too much."

His father was a coward. Sebastien could see that more clearly each time he marked another year's passing on the wall post outside his room. His father did not take a throne because he was frightened of the price magic required. Of course magic demanded something in return. But a wise man could still win at the game, and that is precisely what Sebastien aimed to do.

After one particular lesson with Iddo, Sebastien asked the prophet, "How long must I wait?"

Iddo did not need any more explanation. "A boy of sixteen can rule a throne," he said, his eyes red around their edges.

So Sebastien waited for his sixteenth birthday with great anticipation.

His father could not see the dark splinters lodged in the blue eyes of his son, for love, alas, is often blind to evil. Love wants to see the person we know lives within, but those we love do not always act like who they really are. And Sebastien had been pulled too deeply into the dark to remember who he was born to be.

So it is that Sebastien's father continued to teach his son all the good magic he knew, continued to drill him on the dark arts Iddo taught, continued to speak words that Sebastien could no longer hear. And Sebastien continued to plan.

And then, on the eve of his sixteenth birthday, after his father had prepared a loaf of spice bread to celebrate and then hung a protective talisman, shaped like a blackbird, around Sebastien's neck, Sebastien stole from the house into the darkest night the land had ever seen.

"For you, mother," he said, and he ran without a single goodbye.

# Change

On the other side of the door stands a bent woman in a red hooded cloak. She carries a basket full of berries that have turned her teeth blue. It is all she has had to eat on her journey of ninety-three days.

She has come from the northern kingdom of White Wind, where a prophecy flew in on the north wind and told her of this journey. A prophetess can only go where she is told, and so she left on her journey immediately, just after sending word to King Willis that she was on her way with a Word. She knows all the lands quite intimately. The lands between Fairendale are lands of plenty, so she left with only a basket, sure that she would find sustenance along her way—berries, plants, mushrooms. She has done well with the berries, though nothing else. The lands, it seems, are not quite as plentiful as they once were.

The kingdom of White Wind is very unlike the kingdom of Fairendale. Though Aleen arrived here when the land had already grown dark, she could see that Fairendale was much more beautiful than the land from which she had come. It was much more colorful, much brighter, much warmer. She did not need to shiver when she crossed into the bounds of Fairendale.

She has not come with the Word King Willis wants to hear. But a prophetess can only deliver the message she has been given, and that is precisely what she will do, for she is a good prophetess, just as she was once a good magician.

She has her own hopes, too. She hopes that she will find a place in this beautiful kingdom so unlike her own, with a king who will be loved by his people.

Oh, yes. She has seen change coming.

Will she find a place among the change?

Perhaps. Perhaps not.

Down below the throne room, in the secret dungeon below the dungeons of the castle, a place so dark one could not see a finger held right in front of one's face, sit one hundred forty-two prophets who have come before this one. There is no light here. There is no warmth here. There is no hope here.

This is a dungeon that needs no guards, only iron bars and walls and a floor made of stone. This far underground, magic is lost, though the prophets do not have magic to begin with, you see. They gave up their magic long ago, when they chose children and then the way of prophecy.

In a dark such as this one, there is no reason for the one hundred forty-two prophets to keep their eyes open. So they mostly sleep. Except for one.

Only one stays awake.

Only one holds to hope.

Only one sees the vision of deliverance stepping across darkness.

"Soon," he whispers to all his sleeping brothers. "Soon we shall all be together. Soon we shall escape."

In the village, Arthur steps into the room Theo and Hazel share. He has come to tell them a story and kiss them good night. Come to smooth their hair and settle their worries and turn down the torches.

But tonight he lingers. Perhaps he senses something.

Perhaps he knows. Perhaps his son is not so clever at lying as he supposes.

Theo watches his father linger. He wonders if his father waits for something. Perhaps he should share what happened in the village today. He does not know what his father will say. He merely knows that this secret is burning his mouth, and he cannot play calm for much longer.

"Papa?" Hazel says. Arthur startles, just the tiniest bit, in a way one would not notice if one were not already looking. But Theo and Hazel are observant children, always watching. "Is something wrong?"

Their father shakes his head. "No," he says, and then: "Only a strange feeling."

Hazel sits up, her hands clasped in her lap. "A feeling?" she says.

Hazel is familiar with her father's feelings. He had a feeling when the first prophet came to town. The prophet disappeared and no one ever knew what was exchanged between him and the king.

Arthur had a feeling when all the other prophets came, too. Perhaps there is yet another.

Hazel looks at Theo. He looks at his hands, rubbing his knees. Her brother made a mistake that could cost his life, if this prophet shares a truth the others did not know. A magical boy who does not yet sit the throne has no hope in a kingdom like Fairendale.

"Papa," Theo says. Will he tell his father? Will he share his mistake? Will he let his father carry this worry for him?

"Yes, son?" Arthur says. He stares out their window, which looks out toward the castle. It is open, inviting the cool breeze inside. The white curtains shift and curl.

Theo tries to keep his voice steady, tries to speak in a way that sounds natural and calm and not terrified as his eyes suggest. "I did something today," he says. He looks at Hazel, who nods. *Go on,* her eyes say. *Tell him.*

Arthur looks at his son, drawn out of his thoughts. He moves to Theo's bedside.

"It was an accident," Theo says. Now he looks at his father. Arthur does not show the slightest bit of worry. He has always been good at hiding these things. It is what one does when one is a parent.

"What did you do, son?" Arthur says, his voice steady and gentle. He takes his son's hand. He does not assume, does not propose his own ending to his son's beginning, does not worry. Yet.

"I…" but Theo cannot finish. He cannot tell his father this.

So Hazel does instead. She sits straight up in her bed,

her purple nightgown swallowing her where the crisp white sheets do not. "He used magic."

Arthur studies his son but does not say anything. They wait.

"To whom?" Arthur finally says, for this matters a great deal.

"To Mercy," Hazel says. Her eyes shift to her brother. She does not want to tell, either, but she knows she must. "And Prince Virgil."

Her father clears his throat. "I see," he says. His children watch him, but he does not say another word, as if there is nothing more to say. But there is plenty more to say, dear reader.

"Does he know?" Arthur says, finally.

"I told a story," Hazel says. Her eyes flicker. "I said I did it."

"But he might," Theo says. "We are not certain."

Arthur pats his son's hand. "Let us not worry ourselves, then," he says, and his eyes say the same. This is the face that reassures his children. Arthur kisses his son's cheek and moves to kiss his daughter. Then he stands and gives a small stretch, his thin body lengthening and flattening until it smooths out again. He walks toward their door.

"Papa," Hazel says when he is almost there. He turns

back.

"Yes, Hazel?" Arthur says.

"Why would Prince Virgil say magic is stupid?"

Arthur lets out a long, deep breath. Its whisper falls on the children's ears like a spell, and they are suddenly very tired. But they must know the answer to this question, too, and everyone knows that when children must know something, they will never be able to sleep until they do.

Arthur leans against the doorway, crossing one foot over the other. The toes of his boots have pulled away from the sole, and his dirty white stockings poke through. There is a crack up high, near the knee. His pale brown pants are streaked with dirt, and his tunic is laced tightly enough so the white shirt on his belly is protected. His sleeves, ruffled at the ends, ripple in the wind.

"Well," he says. "There could be many reasons."

Many reasons, perhaps. But he knows the one. Because it has to be the one. Yet Arthur has a duty to his children, to dispel their fears so they can find rest.

"It could be that the king and queen forbid him from practicing magic outside the castle, and he does not like their rules. Or perhaps they do not wish him to practice it until he is of a certain age." The children nod. Parents in the village are not quite as strict with their children as a king and queen must be. None of the village children will rule a throne, after all. Arthur continues. "It could be that he is having trouble in his studies and his magic is not working the way he thinks it should. In which case, perhaps we could help." He looks at Hazel as he says the words.

Arthur's eyes grow cloudy then, as if he is not in the room with them at all. "It could be that he does not have the gift of magic."

The words do not come easily. Arthur, you see, remembers another boy who said those very words when he was a child. He remembers trying to help and being cursed away. And even though he knows these words will not make his children feel any better, he also knows that he must tell them the truth. He simply must.

Hazel and Theo look at him, their eyes wide.

"Surely not," Hazel says. "Why would Prince Virgil not have the gift of magic?" She looks at her brother, as if begging him to agree that this cannot be so. "I thought princes were always born with magic."

"Not always," Arthur says. "There are rules to magic. Only firstborn children get the gift."

"But Prince Virgil is an only child," Hazel says.

"Yes," Arthur says. "He is." He uncrosses his legs and crosses his arms instead. "Then I suppose we have nothing to worry about, do we?"

"But if he does not have magic," Theo says. He lets the sentence hang in the room, where it twirls on the wind.

Arthur looks at Theo. His eyes hold something different now, something wild and haunting and terrifying. It makes Theo catch his breath. "Well, then, Prince Virgil would have something to lose if someone knew his secret," Arthur says. "And a boy with magic would be in grave danger." He clears his throat. Hazel shifts her gaze to her father now.

"So Theo—" she says, but her father shakes his head. She stops.

"Theo is a boy," her father says. "A boy without magic." Then softer, "You understand."

Theo and Hazel nod. "Yes, father," they say.

"Goodnight, then," Arthur says. "I love you both dearly."

They echo his words, and then Arthur moves silently through the shadows, into the bedroom he shares with his wife. Maude is bending over a wash basin, candlelight flickering across her brown dress. Arthur does not say a word. He moves behind Maude and puts his arms around her and holds tight, so tight she turns.

"What is it, Arthur?" she says, her dark eyes troubled.

Arthur shakes his head, buries his face in her silvery

brown hair. He has no words for the cold terror that has crept up his arms and legs and sent its ice storm straight to his heart.

He never should have returned. He never should have risked it. He never should have followed his heart back to the people he loved. He knew something like this could happen. He knew they could not stay here forever, hiding a secret as important as this one.

So they will have to run. They will have to go. They will have to find a place, somewhere safer than here.

The morrow. They shall leave in the dead of night. They shall escape.

They shall live.

"Come in!" The king's voice crawls beneath the gap between the door and the marble floor. The prophetess straightens her back as well as she can. But it is not much, you must understand, for she is an ancient woman. She hitches up her robe and steps through the door opened by a man in balloon pants. "Thank you," she says. He bends his head, just slightly, the only acknowledgment that he has heard the words. He remains outside. She limps in.

"Ah," King Willis says. "Ah ha ha." His arms are

stretched out, as if waiting for an embrace. But this is not the way of the king, and she is still a long distance from the throne. She knows of this king and his ways. He merely believes she is here to deliver the Word he would like to hear, the Word he sent in his letter that reached her on her travels. The king believes she can gift his son with magic though he was not born with it. This hope makes him generous.

The queen waits at the bottom of the steps, along with a handsome boy dressed in a cape and tunic and boots very like his father's, black, trimmed with gold near the knees. His dark eyes watch her approach, and her dark eyes watch him. This is the boy she has seen in her visions. This is the boy who will set it all in motion.

Prince Virgil, in return, stares at her ebony skin and the hair that is wrapped in gray-black braids that swing with every step so it looks as if serpents sit on her head. She is frightening, and yet something about her is familiar. He has never seen her before. But perhaps he has read about her in stories. He once took a book on prophets and prophetesses from his father's library. Perhaps she was in it.

"Your name," the king says when she has hobbled close enough to the throne.

Our prophetess stops on the carpet. He waves her still

nearer. She waits until she is closer to answer his question, which annoys our king. He is not a king accustomed to waiting, after all. "My name," she says, straightening up her bent back as well as she can manage, "Is Aleen. Aleen of White Wind."

Prince Virgil studies her closer. Yes. He has seen her picture in the book. Aleen of White Wind is the most famous prophetess in history. She was born more than a hundred years ago. One hundred forty-two years, to be precise, but Prince Virgil was never a boy bent on precision. He could complete his studies "well enough" so he could spend the rest of the afternoon in the village, playing. He could lace his tunic "well enough" before venturing past the castle walls. He could learn to ride a horse "well enough" before dismounting and racing off to his friends. His tutors know well his shortcomings. They tolerate them but try not to encourage them.

Prince Virgil did not know a prophetess this old could still be alive. He looks at his mother. Queen Clarion grips his hand but stares at the prophetess.

Surely Aleen has brought them good news. Surely a woman so famous from the faraway land of White Wind would come with news that would not send her to a dungeon.

"What Word do you bring me?" the king says.

"A Word of magic." Aleen's voice creaks on its way out. Hundreds of wrinkles slice and twist across her dark face. They ripple and fold when she speaks, as if the family of serpents has moved from her hair to her cheeks.

"A Word of magic!" the king bellows. "Pray tell me then, woman."

She smiles. Prince Virgil stares. She looks a thousand years younger when her white—or are they blue?—teeth are showing. She is not missing a single one, which is quite remarkable in one so ancient. Aleen keeps her teeth strong by eating apples. Three a day, to be exact, though she has not had one since she set out from White Wind.

"There is a boy," the prophetess says. She looks at Prince Virgil. His heart thumps hard. Could it be him? Could he have magic they have not yet discovered? Could he be the real heir to the throne after all? Aleen turns back to the king. "A boy with magic."

If one were to turn one's attention from the prophetess to the queen, one would see Queen Clarion squeezing her son's hand, beaming into his face with a look that says, "See? There is hope still." For a mother will always hope where her child is concerned.

Oh, sweet queen. Poor, sweet queen.

"My son!" King Willis says, and there is no room left for disagreement. "You have come to awaken his magic." The words hang in the air, shifting on their breaths, an impossible command.

Aleen throws her head back, her hair swinging again, and lets out a hoarse laugh. It is quite disturbing and a bit exaggerated. It has been so long since she has laughed, you see, so she is out of practice. The laughter makes her insides feel warm. When she is finished, she looks at Prince Virgil. Her eyes are nearly black, and he takes a step back, unprepared for that empty look, the look all prophets get when they are seeing a vision. She licks her cracked lips. She gives a vicious shake of her head. "I cannot awaken magic," she says. "One is born with magic."

"You must do this awakening!" the king roars.

"I cannot," Aleen says, still shaking her head. Prince Virgil turns away. "It is already too late."

"Then who is this magical boy?" The king's voice rumbles through the throne room, bouncing off the walls and beating his audience with its echo.

"I cannot tell you who," Aleen says. "But I can tell you where."

The king waits, but he is not a patient man. And when the silence stumbles on for too very long, he says, "Where?"

in a voice that could shake the walls were they not made of the sturdiest stone.

The prophetess holds up a bent finger, pointing out the window behind the king. The window that looks upon the village of Fairendale.

"The village?" the king says, turning to look. Prince Virgil cannot take his eyes off the woman's finger and its dirty, curved nail. That one finger holds more power than he could ever hope to have, though this prophetess has no magic.

"Yes," Aleen says. "There is a boy in the village who was born with the gift of magic."

Prince Virgil's face begins to burn. He knows who it is. He knows the boy with magic. But he is a best friend. Best friends do not betray one another. Best friends keep even the most dangerous of secrets. Best friends…

"And what else have you seen?" the king says. "What else do you know?"

Aleen creeps closer to the king's throne. She does not fear a man like him. Prince Virgil feels his heart beat faster. "I have seen destruction," she says. "I have seen death. I have seen a throne in ruins."

"No," the king says. "It cannot be."

"Yes," Aleen says. "Oh, yes."

The king's face has turned ashen. He is staring at the back of the throne room, toward the doors. Prince Virgil watches his father and feels as if he is losing either way. Keep the secret and make his father worry. Share the secret and perhaps endanger the life of his best friend.

What would happen to Theo? Would he be imprisoned? Would he be killed?

A friend cannot do that to another friend. So our prince remains silent, for now.

"When?" the king says now. "When will what you have seen come to pass?" His face is red and splotchy again. His boot stamps the floor, as if he is an angry, petulant child. His hands grip the throne so hard the gold cuts marks into the flesh of his palm.

"Soon." Aleen's voice scratches against the walls. "Soon. Very, very soon."

King Willis flicks his wrist, a small movement that throws open the door of the throne room and sends footsteps running, men's boots cracking against the marble floor. Garth stands before the king, bowing deeply. "Yes, m'Lord," he says.

"Find the captain," King Willis says. "Bring him here."

Garth bows again. "Yes, Your Most High King." He scurries out again.

Everyone in the throne room holds their breath until the captain of the King's Guard, a man called Sir Greyson, stands before the king with his sword point against the marble floor and his hands crossed upon the hilt. The candles flicker against the metal armor the captain wears at all times.

Queen Clarion tries to pull her son toward the door, but Prince Virgil shakes her off. He wants to hear what will happen. He has friends in the village, after all.

King Willis shakes himself out of his throne and paces back and forth across the stage, in heavy, lumbering steps. "There is a boy, captain," he says. "A boy in the village. A boy who has magic." He turns around and paces the other way. "This is a danger to us." He stops and looks at his captain. And it is only because Sir Greyson has removed his silver helmet that the king can even see the grey-blue of his eyes, though he is not paying attention enough to notice color. He is quite thoroughly distracted by this news he has been given. I am sure we can all empathize with our king. If one receives news one was not expecting, it can throw a whole evening off balance.

"So," King Willis says. He turns back to the window that faces the village. "Something must be done. The village must be searched, its people punished."

"Wait," Prince Virgil says. There is an easier way. Theo will give himself up, if he knows everyone else in the village is in danger. Prince Virgil knows he will. "Wait, Father."

King Willis turns to him, as if surprised his son is still here, or, perhaps, that he has a son at all. "We will invade every territory from here to the kingdom of Guardia," the king says. "We will leave no stone unturned. We will find the boy with magic." His eyes grow suddenly soft. He looks at Prince Virgil as if he really sees him this time. Moments of fatherhood can turn the most spindly men into the gentlest creatures, though King Willis has never been a gentle father. Or a concerned one, for that matter.

But this, a magic boy threatening his son's reign, this has turned him uncharacteristically gentle. "You will keep your kingdom, son," he says. He even strides over to Prince Virgil and pats his head. Prince Virgil stares at the red carpet, uncomfortable with this attention.

"Wait, Father," he says, still staring down rather than up. "I know something."

"You know something?" his father says. The king grows impatient again, and just like that, the tender spell is broken. Children, you see, at least according to King Willis, are better seen and not heard. "What could a boy like you know?"

"I think I may know," Prince Virgil says. "I think I may know the boy with magic."

Should he tell? Should he betray his friend? Should he do it in the name of safety for all the others? Does our prince care enough to risk the life of his friend so he can save the lives of Hazel and Mercy?

Yes. Yes, he will tell.

The room grows absolutely still. Only the swishing of Queen Clarion's skirts as she draws nearer to her son and the raspy breath of the prophetess can be heard above the stillness.

Queen Clarion places her hand on her son's arm. Does she know about the boy, too? Perhaps she suspects. Perhaps she has no idea. "Are you sure, Virgil?" she says. Her eyes hold warnings, as if this is a leap forward one could never take back. The queen knows about leaps forward that appear to be solutions but are really only disasters. She lived through her own, many years ago.

But Prince Virgil does not heed his mother's warning. He simply says, "Yes."

"Who, son?" King Willis says. "Who is the boy with magic? Where does he live?"

"The boy with magic is Theo," Prince Virgil says. "He is the furniture maker's son." Queen Clarion gasps.

"And how do you know, boy?" King Willis says.

"I saw him do magic," he says. "His sister tried to cover it up, but I could tell. He made a puppet fall out of the sky and land in his hands."

Queen Clarion puts her hand over her lips, as if she can change the betrayal of this gaping secret by stuffing it back into her own mouth. But it hangs in the air, and it makes King Willis laugh—a loud laugh that echoes all through the chambers, that would surely shake the foundation of a home as humble as Arthur's but cannot touch the solid one of the palace.

"The furniture maker's son," King Willis says. "Well, now, that is interesting." He moves back to the throne and squeezes into it once more. "That is interesting indeed."

The room waits for what comes next. They all know that something is next.

"We shall attack this night," King Willis says. "While they sleep. We shall move in with cages and swords and teach them all an important lesson they will never forget."

"But," Prince Virgil says. "But there is only one."

King Willis turns black eyes to his son, his brows drawn tight over them. "How old is your friend, son?"

Prince Virgil swallows. "Eleven," he says, sure he knows where his father is going.

“Eleven,” King Willis says. His eyes grow ever darker. “Eleven years they have hidden a boy with magic. An entire village has done it. An entire village will pay.”

“No,” Prince Virgil says. “No. Please, Father.”

“Silence!” King Willis says. “I will not have a boy arguing with a king!” He looks at Queen Clarion. She takes Prince Virgil’s hand and pulls him toward the doors again. He shakes against her, but this time her grip is sure and strong. She gets him all the way out the door and into the great hall before he collapses in her arms.

She holds him as long as she dares.

Sir Greyson did not ask to be here. Not really. Captain of the King’s Guard is a position he inherited from his father, when the brave man was killed by the red rain of an exploding mountain during a routine trip to the kingdom of Ashvale, a mostly peaceful land. The King’s Guard is put in place to ensure the safety of the royal family, but part of that safety is assured through routine trips to distant lands, where kings and queens are given not gifts of gold or silver but flower seeds, for the beauty of Fairendale is revered throughout all the lands. Many a kingdom aspires to be as colorful as this one.

Sir Greyson's father was killed when a Fire Mountain in Ashvale erupted and set the whole town smoking. He went back to save its people, of course. He died instead. When his men brought the tragic news, they knelt at Sir Greyson's feet and said they would follow him anywhere, though he was merely a boy of seventeen.

He did not want to be a soldier for a king like King Willis. He would gladly have turned it down, but his mother, dear reader, was stricken by the sugar sickness. She was near dead. And the only way to acquire her medicine, you see, was to work for the king. This is the way of Fairendale, under the hand of King Willis, though it all began with his father, King Sebastien. It is not always fair. But justified, according to King Willis. And that is all that matters to him.

But this. This attacking a village full of people he loves is not something Sir Greyson can do.

"Are you sure it is wise to attack the entire village, sire?" Sir Greyson says. King Willis turns angry eyes to his captain. Sir Greyson shrinks a bit, glad he is wearing armor, though it is silly to think the armor will protect a heart from the vicious words of men. Nothing protects a heart but a wall. And Sir Greyson has never been one for building walls, only opening doors. He is known throughout the village as an honorable man. The widows call him an enviable son.

"Of course I want to do it," King Willis says, as if Sir Greyson's question is the silliest question he has ever heard. Who is Sir Greyson to argue with a king? "The people of Fairendale must know that their king will not tolerate secrets. They must be taught honesty." The king puffs himself up, sticking his great belly out further, if it is possible. "They must be taught integrity. They must be taught honor."

Sir Greyson does not ask any more questions, though he wonders what the village people might have to say about honesty and integrity and honor if they knew the secrets King Willis whispered in this room where he thought there were no ears. There are always ears in a palace.

Oh, yes. Sir Greyson knows why the king is terrified of a magical boy. He has heard more than he should.

But his mother. He cannot refuse the king. He cannot tell the people what is coming. He cannot let his mother die, which she will surely do without the medicine the king's page hands him every evening.

In fact, Sir Greyson is waiting on that medicine as we speak. He is wondering, while the king is laying out his elaborate plans, if his mother is feeling well or if she has taken to her bed. Will he find her sleeping when he shows himself home? Will he find her cooking a late supper? Will he find her reading that storybook she used to read aloud when he was just a boy, the only storybook she has ever had?

The king's voice stops. Sir Greyson looks up. The king is watching him. "This night," King Willis says. "You will take them tonight."

"Them, sire?" Sir Greyson says.

"Yes," King Willis says. His voice bounces off the walls and back at Sir Greyson, like a hard ball. "Round up all the children in the village. Bring them here."

"But is there not only one who has magic, sire?" Sir Greyson says. "A boy?" What would he want with all the young ladies? Sir Greyson has seen them doing magic in the streets, of course, but young ladies have no power in Fairendale. They are no danger.

He does not mean to question his king, this captain of the guard. It is just that he loves the village and its people, and he does not want to frighten or hurt anyone unnecessarily.

But the king cares nothing for caution such as this. His eyes narrow. He points them at Sir Greyson. "There are many ways to hide magic," he says. "A boy could become a girl. A young man could become a child. There are many ways." He takes a deep breath, as if this line of speech has winded him. "Bring them all." His belly shakes into a laugh. "Bring them all. We will find the one."

"And you would have us to take them this night?" Sir Greyson says.

"This night," King Willis says. "You shall round them up this night."

"But it is late, sire," Sir Greyson says. "My men have already retired to bed." It is a lie, of course. The king's men are always ready for action. But Sir Greyson needs some proper time to think. Some time to process what is being asked of him. Some time to decide that his mother's life is worth more than this treachery.

The king is watching him. There is no bottom to the blackness in his eyes. Sir Greyson knows the king well enough to know that his eyes tell the story of his emotions. The darker they grow, the angrier the king. He represses the urge to take a step back, away from those holes. "Then we will round them up at dusk tomorrow," the king says. "What is a few hours? You will take them when they are all watching the day's end. When the only thing on their minds is turning in for the night."

When they least expect it. The people will least expect something like a roundup when they are sitting comfortably in their chairs, hoping to see a mermaid's tail.

He would warn his mother, but what would she say? Would she forbid him to do such a thing? Would he have to watch her die because of it?

He will tell no one.

He has sworn his allegiance.

He is a man of honor.

What does honor mean in a circumstance such as this one?

Sir Greyson simply nods his head. He tries not to think about the boy with magic in a kingdom as peaceful as Fairendale, a boy who has hidden all these years and never raised a bit of a threat. Is he foolish to believe his king is mad? Is he foolish to think that a boy with magic would keep a pure heart free of invasion dreams in a kingdom as wondrous as this one? Is he foolish to wonder, for just a moment, whether the boy might be the relief the kingdom needs after the reign of King Willis and his father before him?

"Make sure they do not hear you coming," King Willis says, as if he knows more about these things than Sir Greyson does. Sir Greyson knows about stealing into the dead of night. He knows about surprise and attack. He knows about war and peace and all the lines in between, for his father taught him when he was but a boy, though he has never seen anything but ease in his duty thus far.

Yet the words give Sir Greyson pause. His men, after all, wear armor that clanks as if they are wearing costumes of broken bells. Perhaps they would have to enter the village without their armor. Suppose they did. Perhaps it would make the people less likely to fight. Perhaps they would simply hand over their children, if Sir Greyson promised they would get them back.

Would they get them back? Is this a promise he can make at all? He does not know what the king plans to do with the children, and Sir Greyson is not a man to make promises he cannot keep.

"And kill the ones who resist." King Willis looks at Sir Greyson. His face breaks into a slow grin, flickering by candlelight so it appears twisted and evil, the face of his father before him. Sir Greyson shudders in his armor.

He does not know if he can do this. He has never killed anyone. He could never kill the people he loves.

He will find another way.

"Page!" the king bellows. The thin boy who is the king's manservant scuttles into the room. "Get the captain his medicine." The king gestures a grand farewell and turns his back to Sir Greyson.

"Yes, sire," Garth says and scuttles back out the door. Sir Greyson waits one minute, two, five, and then Garth returns, with a bottle in his hands. Only then does King Willis turn back around.

"This one," King Willis says. He points to the old woman, standing in shadows beside the throne. "Take this one to the dungeons. With all the rest."

Sir Greyson stares for a moment at this woman ancient and bent, this woman who reminds him of his mother, only older. She looks at him with the blackest eyes he has ever seen, blacker even than those of King Willis, only they are kind where the king's are hard. She gives the slightest nod of her head, sending her braids roving.

Just before he hands her over to Calvin, the boy who feeds the prisoners, he hears the prophetess murmur, "It has begun."

The words send chills down his back.

## Promises

Sebastien had an army of twenty thousand men when he reached the bounds of Fairendale. There were many who would work for the promise of grandeur and honor and wealth in a kingdom as rich and beautiful as Fairendale. It was not so very difficult to build his army of young, strapping men.

King Brendon had ruled for many years, but all in the kingdom knew that he had no gift of magic, that he had only a daughter as heir to the throne. They knew, also, that they loved him dearly. He was a good king, kind and true and so very generous that no man, were he born with magic in the very kingdom he could steal, would ever want to challenge one such as him. He was not particularly skilled in sword fighting or combat strategy, but he was particularly skilled in loving his people and caring for them well. A kingdom can flourish more beneath a king who cares than beneath a king who does not.

But Sebastien was only a boy. He did not know the stakes.

He only knew that he was powerful and there was a kingdom ready to be stolen from the hands of the king with no magic to match his own. He knew, also, that he had another magic more powerful than most: charm. How does one build a twenty-thousand-man army without charm? How does one win the hearts of mothers and wives in foreign kingdoms so they willingly permit their men fight, without charm? How does one convince men to leave their wives and children and follow him into danger without charm?

Sebastien had traveled to the lands of White Wind in the north and Eastermoor in the East and Ashvale in the West and Rosehaven in the northwest. The only land left untouched was Guardia, to the far, far north, simply because he knew its people would be immune to all his charms. He did not need a trip to foreign lands as harsh as that when it would only prove pointless. Sebastien, you see, also had the gift of combat strategy.

When he had finished gathering men from distant lands, Sebastien returned to Lincastle, to all his friends, and he invited them to fight for his cause. The kingdom of Fairendale never saw him coming out of Lincastle, though his numbers were great. Fairendale was peaceful, and sometimes years of peacefulness can make a king let down his guard.

And Sebastien had mastered the concealment spell. Though it weakened him considerably, he risked his own life to ensure that the people of Fairendale and their dragons of Morad did not see or hear his men coming. He grew tired toward the end. A dragon spotted them when the spell left a hole in their fog. But it was already too late. Sebastien and his men had already invaded the land.

Sebastien marched his men through a burning forest. Men screamed around him, writhing, falling, dying, but he did not stop. He was untouchable. The talisman his father had given him for his sixteenth birthday served him well that day. Archers brought down dragons all around him. He watched them fall, and he marveled at this army he had built. He was a king. That much was certain.

Sebastien was the first to step into the clearing, where he found a wall of people surrounding the king's castle. But they were untrained men, not so very difficult to cut down.

He did offer them the opportunity to surrender peaceably. He would never have let them all go, of course, but they did not take the chance to test his word. They attacked, so his men, what was left of them, attacked as well.

King Brendon headed straight for Sebastien. The king's scream filled the whole world. "I am the one you desire," he said. "Please take me. Let my people go." But it was war, and one could not simply let people go, not when swords clashed all around and scarlet stained the once-green grass and Sebastien's staff did its work. The castle grounds and all around it grew quiet, eventually. There were heavy losses on both sides. Only a handful of villagers remained. They gathered together in a tight circle on the lawn of castle, bleeding from wounds that would heal. His men gave a shout of victory, though it was not a loud one, for their side had lost many as well. Sebastien suspected some of them had deserted in the heat of battle.

Sebastien smiled, a dashing kind of smile that made some of the village ladies swoon, he could tell.

"If you swear your fealty to me," he said, "I will let you go." This time he meant it. He needed ladies and gentleman in the kingdom, for he needed to rule over someone. These who remained were the bravest and smartest of all the kingdom's people, he supposed. They did not say a word, but he knew they were simply too afraid to speak, or, perhaps, too awed. Sebastien ordered what remained of his men to let them go, and then he broke through the heavy oak doors and the spacious halls and walked the royal carpet to the golden throne.

And when he had settled into the cushioned chair rimmed with gold and jewels, he smiled another dashing smile, though no one was in the room to see it, and gently set his staff on the ground, to do its deepest work yet.

If one had been standing in the ring of villagers still living, one would have seen every man who had followed Sebastien across rivers and mountains and grasslands fall down around them, to never rise again. A king did not have to fulfill his promises after all.

# Friends

It is still dark when Hazel slips out to tend the sheep.

She tends them every morning, this gentle girl of twelve, for though the sheep do not belong to her, they love her and trust her and know that her pockets are perpetually full of treats that she is always generous enough to share, though food is precious in the household of Arthur and Maude. Sheep are not dull creatures, contrary to popular belief, and they sense her sacrifice. They love Hazel for it, watching from the fields, bleating out their call that will gather the flock and welcome her to them, a call that sounds a bit like "Bo Peep." They watch for her every morning, awaiting her hand's tender touch, awaiting the click of her tongue, awaiting the soft voice that invites them to eat before they nuzzle up to her and take what she has to give them.

They know the sound and smell of their shepherdess, and they trust her completely.

Most of the village people have not yet risen. Only a few houses, where mothers take to the kitchens, kneading the bread they will put in the oven for the mid-day meal, if they have enough flour to bake (many do not), light the still-dark world. The kingdom has been ailing for a time, where food is concerned. The villagers share what they have, but some families, of course, need more than others. Sadly, they do not always get it.

The village, though, has a gardener, and at least there are fresh vegetables for every family every day. Sometimes Maude slices them all into a hearty vegetable stew. Sometimes she steams them in a pot, and Hazel and Theo have carrots and cauliflower and broccoli for dinner. Sometimes, on occasion, there is a roast leg of lamb, when Hazel can bear to part with one of the village sheep. She prefers not to choose or to know which one it will be, begging the butcher to do this work himself, though she always knows which is the missing one. A shepherdess would always know a thing like that.

Mostly the sheep are used for their wool coats, harvested so that Maude and the other village women can spin their fur into yarn and knit the children warm caps and gloves and sweaters for the cooler mornings that come around once every year, for only a month or two.

Hazel stares up at the moon, low in the sky, as if it is setting at the same moment the sun is rising. She loves this still quiet, when the whole world holds its breath before the start of a new day.

"Come, my sweets," Hazel whispers to her sheep. "Let us find water."

The sheep roam close to the Weeping Woods, where no villager has been brave enough to go since the days King Sebastien stormed the throne with twenty-thousand men, many of whom died in those woods and are said to haunt them still. Fairendale parents urge their children to keep their distance from the dangers of the wood, sprites and wood nymphs and goblins and fairies among them. Years ago a child disappeared into the woods and never returned. When her father went to find her, he never returned either.

Hazel tries not to look at the woods as she moves the sheep toward the cove of fresh water just off the road that leads to the castle. She does not wish to see its dark trees, for they look like people standing guard, as King Sebastien's men must have looked all those years ago. She does not wish to see those branches that look so much like arms, reaching toward her.

But her flock gives her courage.

They reach the cove, quiet and tranquil in the morning's chill. Only the first hints of day have begun to peer from the east, where the sky turns a bit less black. Hazel does not approach the water, for she does not want to see whether the mermaids are here or not. Hazel does not like it when they are. Though they seem to enjoy the village boys, mermaids are not often kind to the girls, jeering and poking fun or hiding beneath the cover of water and showing their animal-like teeth to those brave enough to look at them shimmering below the surface. She has had quite a fright other mornings. She does not wish to see the mermaids again, not when she is alone, not even for a glimpse of the tail, the most coveted of luck charms in the village of Fairendale. Hazel cares nothing for luck charms this morning—though one might remember that Hazel looked for the mermaid's tail in the evening past, as every other villager did. Mermaids are easier to enjoy when one is not alone—or very near them.

Hazel watches her sheep drink for a time, careful not to look at the water, where she is certain the mermaids have by now gathered for their morning laugh. Every now and again one of the sheep wanders over to her, and she strokes its curls absentmindedly.

Hazel has many other things on her mind.

Last night's sleep, you see, was filled with nightmares that felt more like real life than just mere dream. One who has experienced a nightmare like this knows how very difficult it is to escape the black cloud of unease that follows one into a morning. And so Hazel broods. Her sheep drink.

One of her favorites, Bluebell, a sheep she named for the tinkling bell tied around its neck and the bluish tint to his wool, approaches her. He nuzzles her arm. He gazes into her eyes, as if he is speaking.

And Hazel, dear reader, understands. It is most astonishing.

"Oh, I do not know," she says. "I simply cannot get that dream out of my head." She picks a piece of grass and watches it twist in the wind. "It was not a dream, really. It was a nightmare."

Bluebell nudges her again.

"I do not wish to speak of it," Hazel says. "It was too horrid."

Bluebell lets out a breath.

"I do not know if I did right," she says. "I do not know if I fully assured them that Theo does not have the gift of magic." She looks at her sheep, scratches his head. "I fear I am not a very good liar." Another sheep near the water lets out a startled bleat. The mermaids have most certainly returned. "They will not believe me."

Bluebell nuzzles her hand. She scratches him more. "I know," she says. "I did my best." Hazel looks at the sky, brightening into a richer blue, like her brother's eyes. "I do not want Theo to get hurt. I have a bad feeling about all this."

Bluebell rests his head on her shoulder. Hazel pulls on a ringlet. "All will be well," she says. She turns to the sheep and takes both sides of his face in her hands. She kisses him right between the eyes. "You are a dear. I always feel better after speaking with you." She whispers the next words. "Thank you."

She stands and taps her staff to the ground. The sheep gather about her, not even needing the rounded end of her staff to draw them closer and tighter. Hazel walks them back to their field, paying no mind to the splash of water and the angry voices of mermaids behind them.

Once the sun wakes the day, Hazel and the girls sit at a great oak table, where cookies are gathered in a bowl.

Every now and again a small hand will reach into the bowl and grab another of Maude's famous pumpkin sugar cookies.

They are listening to Arthur lecture about the dangers of magic. He has followed the trail of danger, after a child asked why the former King Brendon did not simply vanish from the danger of King Sebastien, so that his life might have been spared. Arthur has told them about the instability of this vanishing spell, how when one tries to vanish from a place of danger to a place of safety, one never knows how they will reappear—or whether they will reappear at all.

But if they do not reappear, where do they go? they ask.

No one knows, for the ones who did not reappear have never been found, Arthur tells them.

And what if they reappear? they ask.

One will not reappear with the same face, Arthur says. One could be years older or years younger or a nobleman or a pauper. There are even tales of the fortunate ones who reappeared taking animal form.

"I would be a bear," says a tiny girl sitting at the end of the table. The children call her Lina, for Thumbelina is a name with four syllables, and most everyone knows that a name with four syllables can grow cumbersome to children.

"Alas, you do not get to choose," Arthur says. "The magic chooses for you. The spell must be handled with the utmost care, avoided at all costs."

He fears that they do not understand the dangers that accompany playing with a spell such as this one. The girls, to tell the truth, are more than a little distracted by the scrumptious goodness of Maude's cookies.

And one is distracted by the boy in the back of the room.

Every now and then Mercy glances back at her best friend's brother. Does he have magic? Does he not? Why would they not tell her if he did? Was she not to be trusted?

Theo's face is dark this morning. It holds only secrets, so she cannot read his eyes. She merely knows that he did not sleep last night, for his eyes are shuttered by blue-black circles top to bottom. He watches his father and does not seem to notice her watching him.

But then he catches her staring. He grins, his whole face lighting up with the simple act of lips pulling toward ears, and she turns quickly back to the front, trying to pay attention.

Why would they not tell her?

"Mercy," Arthur says. "What say you show us how to

do a simple transformation spell?" He holds up a dish towel that was draped over the wash basin. "Turn this into a shoe."

"Arthur." Maude snaps the towel out of Arthur's hand. "Not my best towel." The girls giggle. Mercy looks at Hazel and grins. They have never been able to execute a simple transformation spell in this house, for in order to transform something into something else, you must have something first. Maude does not allow for the transformation of her household items, for her house, as is the case with most houses in the village, has only what is absolutely necessary in it. Extra would be lavish. Sometimes, though, the children are fortunate enough to turn an old, tattered shoe into something like a new towel. In fact, Mercy is quite sure a shoe is what this towel used to be, judging by its leathery smell and a hint of, well, foot.

Why would not one simply reverse the transformation spell? That is one of the first questions Mercy asked Arthur back when he began teaching the village girls how to use their magic. "An object can only be transformed once," he said. "If you turn a shoe into a towel, a towel it must remain. Use your transformation magic wisely."

She always had.

Arthur must have forgotten that this towel was a shoe

once upon a time. Mercy's spell would not have worked anyway.

"How about this?" one of the girls says. She holds up her shoe. A giant hole stretches across the toes. The girl has raven black hair and pretty red lips and carries the name Ursula. She is Hazel and Mercy's age, or very nearly, and is known for teasing the mermaids in the cove, dipping her feet into the water and racing back out before they can latch on to her limbs and drag her down to their depths. She makes them dreadfully angry, for they enjoy pulling victims, particularly females, down to their deaths. "I shall go barefoot."

"That is the spirit," Arthur says.

"But dear," Maude says. "What about her mother?"

"The shoemaker is making new ones," Ursula says. She grins at Maude, and there are dimples in both her cheeks and the middle of her chin. Mercy has never really noticed her before. She is a pretty girl.

Arthur looks at Maude, as if asking, "Well?"

"Oh, go on then," she says. The children laugh again. They love to see Maude and Arthur in their home, as much for their kindness as for the love that passes between them. Mercy wonders if she will love her husband someday as Maude loves Arthur. Likely not, as her mother has promised her to Prince Virgil. Only the village girl with the strongest magic is raised to be a queen. Mercy shudders. Perhaps she should have hidden her powers to avoid marrying a boy like Prince Virgil.

"Very well, then," Arthur says. "Can you turn this shoe into a rose?"

She would do better than that, of course. Magic like hers could do much more than a mere rose. She could make the whole bush. And that is exactly what she does, reader. It is really quite amazing. The bush falls into her hands, pricking a couple of her fingers, but she pretends not to notice. The bush is full and lush and beautiful, with thousands of pink roses blooming. Arthur applauds. Mercy bows and tosses the bush so it lands in front of Hazel.

Some of the girls roll their eyes, but Hazel claps. "Beautiful!" she says, as enthusiastic as her father. Even Maude appears impressed. Mercy does not dare look at Theo.

Why did they not tell her?

"You were made for a queen," Arthur says, and, just like that, though it was entirely unintended, Mercy grows melancholy once again.

Yes. She is made for a queen, and that is exactly what they will make her. But she does not want to marry a boy as horrid as Prince Virgil, even if it shall make her queen.

"Yes," Hazel says. "You are powerful enough and beautiful enough." Hazel pats her friend's arm and smiles into her eyes.

Mercy does not want to be powerful and beautiful enough. She merely wants a happy life living among her friends, practicing magic when it suits her. She wants to stay in this warm kitchen with pumpkin sugar cookies forever. She wants to be a village girl with powerful magic.

But we know, reader, that one does not always get what one wants. This is the way of life.

# Blackbird

Soon after taking over the throne of Fairendale, King Sebastien found a beautiful wife, from the kingdom of Eastermoor, known for its beautiful women and strapping young men. His wife was said to possess a powerful gift of magic, though she never used it in front of him. She never did much of anything in front of him but smile demurely and dip her head. She was precisely the kind of wife a man such as King Sebastien desired.

There were men in her own village who wanted to marry a woman as beautiful as Vivian, but her father gave her willingly when a throne was involved. King Sebastien admired her wild red hair and did not care whether she loved him or not. He merely needed a queen with magic to prove he was a king with staying power, passing along the gift to his sons and securing the throne for another generation.

Not that King Sebastien was at all interested in any generation but his own. He did not, in fact, wish to have children. Children were what stole the gift of magic from a man, after all. He had taken the kingdom as a young man of magic, and he desired more than anything to hold on to that magic for as long as he could. He did not wish to become vulnerable as had that old man King Brendon.

And he would not have chosen children at all but for an old, bent prophet who traveled to the kingdom wearing eyes that looked vaguely familiar to our dear King Sebastien, as if he had seen them before. But King Sebastien had met many a man over the years of his life and could not be expected to remember where he had met the one. The prophet seemed to know much about him, as is expected of prophets. King Sebastien did not fear the man. Not until he croaked out in an ancient voice as bent as his back: "Soon you will die, Your Majesty."

His words startled King Sebastien. Surely a man as powerful as he was had many more years to live. Surely he would rule the throne until he was old and grey and wrinkled. But no man or woman in the kingdom of Fairendale, nor in any other kingdom, no matter how powerful, has ever been so powerful as to prevent death.

"Die?" King Sebastien said. They were alone in the throne room. King Sebastien had dismissed all the servants when the prophet asked to speak with him privately.

"Yes," the old man said. "You shall die."

King Sebastien cocked his head. "And how shall I die?" he said. "By your hand?"

"No," the old man said. "Of course not, Your Majesty. You will die by a blackbird's beak."

King Sebastien drew in a sharp breath. He would not have believed something as preposterous as this had it not been for the nightmare he had had since he was a boy. In it, a bird chased him, relentlessly, hungrily, unmercifully. He could never escape from it, but he always woke before it landed upon his face.

He never knew what to do with that dream, but now, with the words of the prophet hanging before him, he felt the dark fog of fear settle over his chest.

"And how will a blackbird kill me?" King Sebastien's voice sounded strangled, as if the blackbird was already doing its work. King Sebastien wondered if the old man was a shape shifter. Would he die, now, in this very room?

"The blackbird," the man said, but he did not finish. He looked into King Sebastien's eyes, and King Sebastien felt a charge of something he could not quite place.

Respect, perhaps? Anger? Recognition. Where had he seen those eyes before? "The blackbird will tear out your eyes and feast on your flesh."

Perhaps it was gruesomely jarring for an old man to tell a king something like this, but this was what King Sebastien had feared his strange dreams were trying to tell him. And so it did not take much convincing for him to believe it.

"What can I do?" King Sebastien said, for a dying man always wants to live. If one had looked into his face at that very moment, one might have seen something one had not seen on King Sebastien's face since he was a boy: Fear.

Perhaps this is what softened the old prophet's heart, what made him tell the only thing left to tell. "Have a child," the prophet said. "This will give you many more years."

"But the blackbird," King Sebastien said.

"It will come," the prophet said. "Once you raise your son."

And so it was that King Sebastien fathered a boy at the age of forty-three. He gave his magic to his firstborn son and had nothing left to give to the one who came a mere ten months later. This is the way of magic. King Sebastien knew the rules, but he thought, perhaps, that by continuing to have children, he could somehow delay his death. Queen Vivian, sadly, died soon after their second son's birth, and he could find no other woman who wanted to marry a man such as him.

No other woman wanted to be a queen?

Being a queen, dear reader, is not so attractive when it means you are forever chained to a disagreeable man. It is better to remain alone in such cases.

King Sebastien raised his two sons, Wendell and Willis, alone. The kingdom knew them as twins. Only he knew them as first and second born.

So it was that the secret began, and to this day remains.

# Death

Prince Virgil did not sleep the entire night. He could not cease thinking about what his father intends to do today. He does not know for sure what his father has planned, of course, but he can guess. A man such as King Willis is not so very hard to read, after all. So in the dead of night, Prince Virgil decided that he would warn his friend on the morrow, and it was only then that he was able to fall into a restless sort of sleep.

Our prince wakes this morning with dread in his heart and a mission on his mind. He dresses quickly, runs to the banquet hall but passes up the sweet rolls in favor of a slice of warm bread and melted butter, for he does not want to be like his father even the smallest bit, and then he races toward the castle entrance at the very moment he hears his father wheezing through the halls. He does not wish to run into his father, you see. He does not want his father to know where he is going.

Prince Virgil slips out, thinking he is unnoticed, though the servants are always watching and listening, at every turn. They have, in fact, seen him today, flying through the castle doors and down the path that leads to the village. They wonder what would make a boy like Prince Virgil, a boy who walks slowly everywhere he goes, run like that. They have never seen him hurry in all his days. The sight of it stills their breath, until they remember he is a boy of twelve. He is a boy. He is twelve. Of course.

Prince Virgil dashes toward the bridge, for once he crosses to the other side, he will be out of the sight of the castle. His father must not see him. He stops to catch his breath on the bridge's safe side, listening for approaching footsteps. There are none.

But there is a voice. It calls out to him. He looks down into the water. He has seen her before, this mermaid, but never so close. He ventures the slightest bit closer.

"Hello, my prince," she says.

"Hello," he says, unsure whether he should move any closer. He is on a mission, after all, and, besides, he knows the dangers of mermaids. He has heard the tales, about how they seduce men into the water and then pull them down into the depths until they cannot take another breath. The tales do not say what happens after that, whether victims turn into mermen or whether their bodies populate the bottom of the Violet Sea, but Prince Virgil is not the boy to find out today.

This mermaid is as beautiful as the rest of her sisters, but where the others are dark, she has white skin and flaming red hair and eyes the color of an evening sky moments before the sun disappears.

Prince Virgil steps closer, without thinking, and then remembers that he plans to stay on dry land. He backs up again.

She is very beautiful, though. The wind twists her hair around her face, and Prince Virgil thinks of Mercy, only this mermaid is ice where Mercy is grass.

"I have seen you before," she says. "Crossing this bridge. Walking into the village."

"Perhaps," Prince Virgil says. He does not mention that he has seen her before.

He takes another step back. He must go. The sooner he can get to his friends, the sooner they will be able to flee. The sooner they shall be safe.

"Why do you go to the village?" the mermaid says. "Those people are not worthy of my prince."

"They are my friends," Prince Virgil says. He turns. He does not know why he stopped on his way. The mermaid's eyes freeze him.

"Do not go, my prince," she says.

"I must warn them," Prince Virgil says, though he does not mean to say these words aloud.

"Warn them of what?" the mermaid says.

"About my father," Prince Virgil says. "What he plans to do." He does not know why he is telling a mermaid this secret.

"But my prince," she says. "It is already too late."

"No," Prince Virgil says. "It is not too late. My father has not given the orders as yet."

"It is too late to undo what has been done," the mermaid says. Her eyes sparkle in the sun. "My father has seen what is to come." Her voice grows softer, as if she, too, is telling a great secret. Prince Virgil takes a step closer, careful to stay well out of the mermaid's reach.

"And what is coming?" Prince Virgil says.

"Destruction," the mermaid says. Her eyes widen. She does not smile. "Death. Do not let the prince get caught up in it all."

"But I must," Prince Virgil says. This brave boy. He knows what it is like to love a boy and two girls. He must do what he can to save them. He turns.

"The kingdom will be taken from my prince's hands," the mermaid says. "Unless…"

She does not finish. But Prince Virgil has heard the important words.

Oh, yes. They have begun to sink down deep.

And instead of running, dear reader, he now walks with measured steps along the road to the village.

He is a boy on a different mission now.

The sun continues to shine brightly in a blue sky, traitor that it is. The sky bears only the smallest spattering of white clouds. It gives no indication that it knows what is coming. One would not even be able to guess, by gazing at this clear, happy display of shining sun and smooth blue, that what is coming is dark and jagged and terrifying.

The somewhat later morning finds the girls of the village still gathered in Arthur and Maude's kitchen. They are still studying magic, this time baking cookies with no hands. Theo watches them, not daring to move after yesterday's mistake. Every now and then Arthur studies his son.

His boy will be happier somewhere else. Somewhere he can use his magic. Somewhere he will not have to hide. Somewhere safe.

Arthur knows precisely the place. He knows precisely the spell. Hazel and Theo and the rest of the gifted children are strong enough to perform the magic necessary to keep the place invisible, but he will have to convince them that they must go.

He does not know how to do this.

The village people love him, for he is good, kind, virtuous Arthur, but they do not understand the urgency he has had over the years, each time a new prophet came to town, for the people do not know the secret he carries.

For a while he believed they were all safe, for all the prophets disappeared and, with them, the danger. But now, after so many years, another has been found.

Another who must have new information for the king.

On the last eve, Arthur stared in the direction of the palace long into the night, watching until the torches went out, but they never did, at least not while he was awake. They remained blazing in the very place he knew the throne room to be. He fell asleep with fear spidering to the corners of his heart.

He told Maude of his plans early this morning, before

Theo and Hazel woke. She wanted to leave before the sun came up, but he could not leave the other children. The king is rash, he knows. If there is a male child with magic, he will capture all the children, male or female, until he finds the one. Arthur, good man that he is, cannot leave the village children to this fate.

Arthur's heart is no longer in magic lessons, though he did well enough in his teaching when the morning began. But every sentence, now, ends in a thought he does not finish. It is Hazel who notices. "Perhaps we should run along and play," she says. Arthur does not argue.

The girls scatter, Hazel and Mercy walking arm in arm and Theo walking behind. All the village boys are busy doing chores, but Theo has already completed his. He rises earlier than most of the others, for he wants to sit in on the magic lessons, though he can never use what he learns. Boys are not permitted leisure time until they finish the village chores. So Theo rises at first light, when he hears Hazel leave her bed. He has never been late to a lesson yet.

Theo spies Prince Virgil walking toward them up ahead. He calls to his friend. When Prince Virgil looks at the three of them, it is as if his brown eyes reach out and strike their cheeks. His eyes are angry and hard, enough to make Theo shiver, enough to make him believe that his friend is very dangerous indeed.

"Want to play with us?" Hazel says, though it is clear by her wide eyes that she, too, has noticed the change.

Prince Virgil does not answer. Instead, he looks behind Hazel, to Theo. Theo, who is looking back at him. Theo, who notices the change. Theo, who suddenly wants nothing more than to run from his best friend.

"What are you doing in the streets already this morning?" Prince Virgil says. "Why are you not doing the village chores like all the rest of the boys?" Prince Virgil sweeps his arm grandly to the side, as if to say, "You see all the others?"

"I finished my chores," Theo says. "I always rise earlier than the rest." He does not want to look at those malicious eyes, does not want to read what is written there. But he does. And the fear crawls up his neck.

Hazel turns to look at her brother. Perhaps she has heard something in his voice. Perhaps she has sensed a change in his breathing. It is difficult to say how twins know the deeper knowings of one another.

"What is it, Theo?" Hazel says. Her eyes study him.

Mercy turns, too.

Theo shakes his head.

Prince Virgil smiles, but the girls are not looking. "I

know what you do, Theo," Prince Virgil says. His smile is wickedly hateful.

Truth be told, he looks just as his father did last night, when he ordered the prophet Aleen of White Wind down to the secret dungeons beneath the dungeons, with the other one hundred forty-two like her.

Why would Prince Virgil, who left the castle walls to warn his friends about his father's plans, suddenly turn against those friends?

Well, reader, desperation makes people do strange things. Many times cruel things, shameful things, things they would never do in a right mind. Despair takes a right mind and twists it until it nearly breaks.

What we do in that breaking moment tells us not who we are but the powerful grip our feelings have on our actions. Prince Virgil, you see, feels confused and angry and desperate. But most of all he feels fearful, for he is a prince, but he is not a prince. He desires a throne, yet he has no claim to a throne. He loves his friend, yet he feels threatened by his friend.

Fear can turn a heart inside out.

See what it does to Theo. See him shake. See the despair hang over him like the heavy clouds gathering in the sky just now. See the sun grow dim, all light hidden behind grey.

"What do I do?" Theo dares to ask.

Prince Virgil takes a step closer. His black boot crushes something beneath it with a snap that startles Hazel and Mercy. "You watch. You learn. Magic."

This is not who Prince Virgil is. This is not the Prince Virgil that Theo and Hazel and Mercy know. He is someone different, someone they do not know and would not like, even a little, if they did.

They all stand in silence, for one heartbeat, two, three, all staring at Prince Virgil with gaping-wide mouths. "I know you want the throne," Prince Virgil says. "But you will never have it." His face grows darker still, and the children, Theo and Mercy and Hazel, take one collective step back. "You will not have it." His words clamber across their necks and chests, beating them in the most tender places.

It is no small sorrow to lose a friend. And that is precisely what is happening. They are all losing a friend. They know this. It is this, not the danger, that leads our brave Theo to speak.

"No," he says. "No, I do not want your throne." His hands move into the air, as if trying to find a rope, trying to pull his body up from the Swallowing Sand that has opened before him. "No."

"Yes," Prince Virgil says. But now his eyes have turned wild and stormy, and the wind has begun screaming, whipping their faces as his words whip their hearts. And then the worst words of them all: "My father knows."

Hazel gasps. A new fear crawls over all of them, squeezing into their aching heads and their dried-out mouths and mostly their quaking hearts.

"I could not take your throne away," Theo says. Remarkably, his voice remains calm. Remarkably, he keeps his head. Remarkably, he loves his friend, still, even after this ugliness. For Theo, you see, is a true friend, though one might argue that a friend who lies to another friend is really no friend at all. "I have no magic."

"But you do," Prince Virgil says. "I saw it." He takes a step closer to the children, his whole face twisted into an ugly sneer. "Yesterday." He points his finger. "Right over there."

"It was I who did the magic," Hazel says. Her voice, unlike her brother's, has turned shrill. "It was I, Prince Virgil."

"Yes, it was you," Prince Virgil says. "That puppet came to him when he held out his hand because you made it."

"Yes," Hazel says. "Yes, of course."

"The only way magic is passed through two is if you are twins," Prince Virgil says. "I have read the magic books." Prince Virgil's cold eyes move from one of them to another, freezing them to their spots on the cobblestone path. His eyes rest on Theo. "Which means Theo has magic after all."

Hazel gasps again, and Prince Virgil's eyes flash in triumph. He has won. He has won this battle, for there is nothing left to say. And no one does, for some very long minutes. The wind speaks for them, shrieking and howling and tearing at their limbs. Who will stand the longest?

"Please," Theo says. "I do not want your throne. I never have."

"You lie," Prince Virgil roars, and the wind comes behind him and picks up his words and lashes them against his friends so they blink and turn their faces away from the force. "You will never have it!"

Prince Virgil turns on his heel, presumably to run off. But he turns back to the children still frozen in fear. "He is coming," he says. He stares at them each in turn, and then he runs with the wind, back up the hill to the palace, while the children stand in a wind that will not die until many more do.

In the kingdom of Fairendale, Death does not come swiftly or easily. He is a man, dressed in black, roaming the streets only when he has become especially hungry for life. The villagers can usually feel him coming, though they cannot see him. At times he stands at a door for days or weeks or months, listening, living through the ones who still live. At times he comes in a great, rapid, unexpected flight and takes as many as he can with one hand, flinging cholera or dysentery or scarlet fever. They are quick and miserable illnesses, and he is always to blame.

He is invisible and unannounced. The living can only feel his cold, rancid breath on their faces.

Today, the village people look at one another. Today they wonder how it will come: quick or many days long. Today they wonder who.

Death is not a welcome guest, to be sure, though the villagers have become accustomed to his presence, for life does not last forever for anyone, not even the people of Fairendale. He is expected and yet unexpected. He is never easy.

If the villagers could see Death, they would, just now,

see him walking into their village, his black robes still and calm, though the wind today is frightful. They would see him move past their houses. They would see him mark the top of a door here and another there. They would wonder if those marks mean what they think they mean.

They would see him lift his hand that is not really a hand but is, in fact, more white skeleton than flesh, and touch the door of Arthur and Maude and Hazel and Theo.

Which will it be? All? None?

Does the mark mean live or die?

There is not time for questions right now, reader.

Death continues moving, continues marking, until he reaches the very center of the village, where the fountain still spouts water, clear and pure.

There he waits.

# Girl

One of King Sebastien's sons grew up good and kind, and reminded him so much of his father that King Sebastien tried to whip the goodness out of the boy. He was the wrong son for this goodness. When King Sebastien caught his son feeding the servants the table scraps he had saved from supper, he took the boy out behind the castle, tied him to a tree and lashed him as many times as it took for the boy to fall to his knees and beg for mercy. He thought the boy had learned, but the boy only grew smarter, and King Sebastien only grew angrier.

The royal boy would give old clothes to the village boys who did not have any while making his village rounds. Soon the villagers gathered out on the road, blurring the line between rich and poor, and King Sebastien was fuming, for he knew his son was to blame. And though he could not prove it, he took his son out behind the castle, again, and beat him, again, until the boy fell to his knees and begged for mercy, and he beat him still more, until the boy could not rise again. Then he returned inside his castle walls and watched from a window as Prince Willis helped his brother to his feet and let him lean on his arm all the way back inside the castle.

It was a bad example for Prince Willis. The boy could not stand to see his brother whipped.

"Do not do it again, brother," King Sebastien heard Prince Willis tell his brother as he hauled him to his bedchambers. King Sebastien was fortunate to have at least one son with common sense. King Sebastien hid in the shadows, which were great about the castle. It was King Sebastien's father who had loved light. King Sebastien preferred the darkness. The better to hide and eavesdrop, which he did that eve.

"I must," Prince Wendell said, his voice shaking. "They are people, too, brother."

"Do not be a fool," Prince Willis said. "Their life is worth nothing to yours."

"Their lives are worth just as much," Prince Wendell said. He stumbled, and his brother helped him to his feet once more. King Sebastien very nearly stepped from the shadows but decided to stay.

"Father does not like it," Prince Willis said. "He will kill you."

"Father will not kill his own son," Prince Wendell said. "His own heir."

"You cannot know that for sure," Prince Willis said. "You must stop this foolishness at once."

"Alas, I cannot," Prince Wendell said. "They are my people, and I love them."

That was the problem. Prince Wendell did love the people. But perhaps if he had another to care for, he would not find as many opportunities to cross his father's line. Perhaps a wife would do him well. A diversion. A gentle voice of reason.

So King Sebastien began to ask around. Who was the most beautiful woman with the greatest gift of magic, a gift fit for a future king?

It did not take him long to find her.

She was just a child, but already she was lovely. A girl from Lincastle King Sebastien did not remember, for she was not yet born when he left. But he knew her family, and they were a good breed. Kind people, it had been whispered, but the father had been a ruthless businessman before he disappeared on a voyage across the Violet Sea, and perhaps the girl had more of the ruthlessness than the kindness. He could do something about the kindness, at any rate. She was just a girl.

What was of more importance to a man such as King Sebastien was her gift of magic. Already, at six years old, the girl was said to be the most powerful girl with magic in all the land. So King Sebastien sent for her.

Her mother did not want to let her go. She was only a girl of six, after all. But in the end, King Sebastien convinced the woman that this was a necessary step for assuring her daughter had a place in the kingdom. His son needed to get to know the girl. They would grow up together for the next ten years, and then they would marry. Her mother, of course, did not dare argue with a king, especially since he paid her handsomely.

The night the girl arrived, King Sebastien threw a great feast in her honor, though none of the villagers were invited. He sat her next to Prince Wendell and sat himself at the other end of the table, where he could watch them both. It was not easy for a nineteen-year-old boy to love a six-year-old, he knew, but this girl would be beautiful by the time King Sebastien was ready to give over his rule of the throne. In another ten years or so. He still had many more years left to him, though the voice of the old prophet had been visiting him of late. Prince Wendell, after him, would have many years of ruling the throne before it came time for him to pass his magical gift to an heir. The throne would be secured forever. This thought brought a smile to King Sebastien's face.

King Sebastien watched the two. Prince Willis was silent, slurping his soup and watching his older brother. Even he could tell the girl was beautiful, King Sebastien knew. With her white hair and her wide blue eyes, startling in their clarity, the girl could steal a stare. She did not talk for the better part of the dinner, and tears swam in her eyes. And then, finally, King Sebastien heard Prince Wendell speak.

"You are a long way from home," Prince Wendell said, and the girl nodded. "It is not easy to be so far from home." King Sebastien watched his son grab the little girl's hand. "You will grow used to it."

The little girl looked up at him, her eyes fixed on his face. She smiled the smallest smile, and there were dimples in both her cheeks, appearing even with such a slight effort.

"I shall take you round the kingdom tomorrow," Prince Wendell said.

The girl nodded. "I would like that very much, thank you," she said, and Prince Wendell smiled at her.

With a girl like this one to care for, Prince Wendell would not have much time for taking care of the villagers, King Sebastien thought.

Yes. It was a very good idea to bring her here.

# Words

In only a few hours, Sir Greyson and his men will move into the village. In only a few hours they will sweep the village of all its children, and possibly its parents, should they decide to fight. In only a few hours Sir Greyson will have to choose between honor and what is right.

And so this is why we find Sir Greyson in the king's throne room, asking once more whether this is what the king wishes to do. For perhaps the king might yet be persuaded to change his mind, having slept on the news of a magical child.

Sir Greyson, on the other hand, knows that what the king asks of him is not right. Last eve he walked the streets of Fairendale in the dark of night, when everything was still and quiet and only the wind talked. And what it whispered to him was, *No. No, no, no.*

But Sir Greyson arrived at his mother's cottage, and she was already in bed, her face white, her hair sticking to her neck and forehead. Her legs were swollen so that when Sir Greyson touched them, his fingers left impressions. He gave her a shot while she slept. She hardly stirred.

She was growing worse. He would need stronger medicine.

So what does a man like Sir Greyson do?

The king is cheerful this morning. He has grand plans for what is going to happen now. Raid the village, in just a few hours, capture all the children, find the one who might steal a throne. The people, of course, will do their duty to the king, for they love and respect and fear him. They revere him. They obey him.

Sir Greyson, however, is not so sure, and that is why his men will wear armor today rather than walk into the village with bare chests and necks and heads.

"Sire," Sir Greyson says. "Are you sure we need all the children? Are you sure we do not need only the children of a certain age group?" Say, ten or eleven or twelve years old? Sir Greyson does not mean to offend his king. So this last bit he keeps for himself.

King Willis licks his fingers. He is eating sweet rolls, of course—his favorite. Sir Greyson wonders if sweet rolls are the king's favorite because of their taste or because there is no other food in the kingdom that so effectively demonstrates the difference between royalty and commoner: Those without means and castles and the barest hint of royalty rarely taste sweet rolls. "Yes, Captain," King Willis says. "I am sure."

"What do we do with their parents, sire?" Sir Greyson says. He does not know if King Willis has thought about what the parents of the village children will do.

"Slay them if they resist," King Willis says.

"But they will all resist," Sir Greyson says. "They love their children."

"Surely they do not all love their children more than they love obedience to their king," King Willis says. "Surely they do not love their children enough to die by the sword." Sir Greyson is not so sure. "And if they do..." The king looks at Sir Greyson. His eyes narrow in his fat face. The cheeks pull up into a smile, like red balls of fluff poking out from a face. "They shall pay dearly for it."

Sir Greyson feels the sickness in his stomach, but he has not been dismissed. So he stands and waits for the king's dismissal. He must watch the king eat three more sweet rolls, stuffing them in his mouth with hardly a chew, before it comes.

"Go," the king says. "Ready your men. It will be dusk soon."

"Yes, sire," Sir Greyson says, and he turns on his heel and retreats to his men.

His mother. What will his mother say when she discovers what he has done?

It is not night, but the day is black all the same. The clouds have rolled in thick and final, as if they know, too, what is to come. Arthur watches them, urging his family to pack faster.

"We must go," he says. "We must leave. Now."

Thunder claps. Lightning flashes on top of thunder.

Maude stares at the sky out the window, at the wind puffing dust in the streets so it is hard to see one house from another. No one moves out of doors. "We will have to wait," she says. Good, practical Maude. She knows they cannot go on in a storm like this one.

"We cannot wait," Arthur says. His voice has become loud, obstinate, raised in fear. "We cannot wait. We must go." He turns to Theo and Hazel. "Children."

Theo and Hazel each carry one bag stuffed with a

change of clothes and some warm bread Maude made in the early morning hours. They will find other food on their way. Or so they all hope.

Hazel's eyes are rimmed with red. She does not wish to leave her friends, but the villagers did not believe Arthur's warnings when he stood in the courtyard earlier today and told them what would come. Not even Mercy will come with them.

Theo's dark blues are wide with worry and regret.

If only he had not used his magic mistakenly. Flight could have been avoided. The lives of the village children would not be in danger.

*I am sorry*, his eyes say, though it is not Theo who needs to apologize. We know who is really at fault here.

"Let us go," Arthur says.

Hazel catches his arm before he walks out the door. "What about the others?" she says. "We must convince them."

Arthur shakes his head. "I have tried, my dear," he says. "They do not listen."

"You must try again," she says.

"There is no time," Arthur says. "We must flee without them."

"You know what the king will do," Maude says. "You

know what will happen."

She has felt Death waiting. He is colder than he ever was.

Arthur stares at his wife. He knows she will not go without this last little try, this thing that is not so very little. He will have to warn them again. He will have to shout above the wind's howl and the thunder's clap. He will have to make them listen this time.

He dips his head.

And then Arthur walks out into the streets, and the wind thrashes his face, and he shouts as loud as he can possibly shout. "Death is coming," he says. "Run while you can."

But the wind, you see, is too loud. The people cannot hear him. They see him in the street, and they come out of their houses and they stand in their doorways, watching, but his words are lost, drowned, stolen by the sound and fury of storm.

And this is why Arthur, Maude, Theo and Hazel stand in the middle of the village street, rather than running. This is why they cannot hear the explosion of a thousand hooves down the road between the village and its castle. This, dear reader, is precisely what destroys them.

When the first horse claps his hoof on the cobblestones

of the village, the sky opens up.

Death waits. Only a few more moments and he will move. Not long now. He has been waiting for hours, but he does not have to wait forever. He will steal his first victim soon.

The first horse emerges from water and dirt and wind, and Death glides from his post.

There will be plenty. Oh, yes. There will be plenty today.

# Banished

There came an evening when taking care of a little girl was not enough for Prince Wendell.

King Sebastien was supping with Prince Willis, for Prince Wendell and Clarion were nowhere to be found when Cook clanged the supper bell. King Sebastien asked questions about their whereabouts, and Prince Willis provided him with unsatisfactory answers, such as, "I do not know" and "He and Clarion went to see the villagers, perhaps," and "Perhaps they went swimming in the cove," and King Sebastien was not a man much given to mercy or mystery. A son late to supper was intolerable. He stormed out of the dining hall, with his youngest son following.

"Father," Prince Willis said. "Father, please. He will be home soon."

King Sebastien turned on his heel and glared at his

son. "You know where they are," he said, and it was not a question. Prince Willis drew back into shadows. King Sebastien pulled him roughly out.

"No," Prince Willis said. "I do not know."

"You do," King Sebastien said. He did not roar. He did not shout. What he did was worse, perhaps. He said the words in a quiet voice, one full of steel and thorns and threat.

For a moment it appeared as though Prince Willis would refuse to take King Sebastien to his brother, for of course Prince Willis knew precisely where his brother was and what he was doing. They were friends and not merely brothers. Prince Willis was forever begging his brother not to visit the village. Prince Wendell was forever begging his brother not to tell.

But King Sebastien tugged violently on a tuft of curls at the nape of his son's neck. He drew his son's eyes to him. "Tell me," he said in that quiet, steely voice. "Tell me, or you will have worse done to you than I have ever done to your brother."

Prince Willis was so overcome by fear that he could do nothing but point the way toward the village. King Sebastien did not have to guess at much beyond that.

But when he came upon Prince Wendell and Clarion,

they were walking along the road back toward the castle. Clarion was holding Prince Wendell's hand. They stopped when they saw King Sebastien on the bridge, Prince Willis several paces behind. Prince Wendell rushed forward, for even at this distance, he had seen his brother's face. Moreover, he had seen his father's face.

"Brother," Prince Wendell said. "What has happened?"

Prince Willis only stared at his father, for he had no words to speak. Prince Wendell turned to his father.

"What have you done?" he said.

"The question is," King Sebastien said, "what have you done?"

King Sebastien did not miss the look between Prince Wendell and Prince Willis, for he was an observant man when it came to wrongdoing. He could spot treachery. He did not miss, either, the way Clarion stared up at Prince Wendell, as if asking how much she should tell this man. Well. There was his way. He would get the child alone, and she would tell all. She would tell all simply because she was a child. "We were visiting our people," Prince Wendell said. "They deserve to see their future king and queen every now and again. Is that not so, Clary?"

Clarion nodded. "We were visiting," she said, though King Sebastien could see the lie her eyes held. She was not so very hard to read, after all.

But once he got her alone, he would discover the truth.

Later that night, King Sebastien stole into the girl's room, though he had never crossed the threshold before. She startled and then bowed her head.

"My king," she said.

"I only wanted to say goodnight," he said. He stood at the foot of her bed.

"Is Wendell coming?" she said. "He usually tells me stories."

"What kinds of stories does Wendell tell you?" King Sebastien said. The child looked small in the enormous bed, white-skinned against the red of her bedcovers.

"Stories of good kings," Clarion said. "Good kings who take care of their people." Her face grew troubled. "You do not take care of your people." She looked stricken for a moment, as though her own words surprised her. Perhaps she had not meant to say them aloud.

"Is that what Wendell tells you?" King Sebastien said.

"Oh, no," Clarion said. "He only says good things about his father." She looked away for a moment and then back at him. "But the people are always hungry. A good king should feed his people."

"Perhaps that is something only a bad king would do,"

King Sebastien said.

“But people should not go hungry—”

“Hush, my child,” King Sebastien said. He sat at the foot of her bed. “Wendell is not coming tonight. I will tell you a story in his place. But first you must tell me a story.”

“But I do not know any stories,” Clarion said. “I do not know how to tell them as Wendell does.”

King Sebastien looked at her golden hair and then back at her face. “You do not have to make it up. You can tell me something that is the truth.”

She tilted her head at him, and he could see the indecision warring between her brows. Should she tell? Should she keep what she carried a secret? He made his move in this elaborate game.

“Tell me a story about what you and Wendell were doing in the village,” King Sebastien said.

The girl hesitated.

“We shall pretend you are telling a story,” King Sebastien said. “I will not know whether you are telling the truth or using your imagination.”

But he would know. Of course he would. She was only a child, after all.

The girl nodded.

It was so easy.

She told him of the village houses and the people they visited, one after another, and the clothes they gave away by turning a sack of dirt into a sweater that would protect a boy from the cold winds of night. She told him of the old shoes turned to food for the people who were nearly starving. She told him of the blankets they made from old castle curtains and the medicine from the castle storehouse delivered to the sick.

And every word of it was true.

King Sebastien, though the anger boiled and belted inside, remained perfectly calm until Clarion had finished her story. When she grew silent, King Sebastien nodded his head. He forced a small smile. "Thank you for telling me a story," he said. "It was a very good one."

And then he swept out of her room, not bothering with his own promise to tell a story. He barreled down the hall and into his son's chambers. His thin veneer of calm was gone before he ever got there. He raged and screamed and said the words he could never, ever take back.

"Get out of my kingdom!"

Prince Wendell watched him, as if he expected his father to take back the horrible words. But King Sebastien did not. So Prince Wendell said, "But father. They are people, too." Precisely what he had told his brother, for he understood, you see, that his father knew his secret, that King Sebastien had pried it from Clarion's lips.

"They are not people," King Sebastien said. "They are workers. They will not work if they have no reason to work. If a king gives them whatever their hearts desire."

"But they are poor," Prince Wendell said. "They do not have enough to eat. They do not have blankets for their beds, for their children. Everything they own is old and threadbare." He took a step toward his father. "Please, Father. They work hard."

"A king is not a wish giver," King Sebastien said. "We do not grant wishes."

"A king cannot idly stand by while his people slowly die," Prince Wendell said. "Tell me, Father, is that what I should do?"

King Sebastien puffed up his chest. He tried to breathe through his flaming anger, but he was much too furious. Too wildly out of control. Too afraid. Why could not the other son, the one who did whatever his royal father asked, be the one born with magic? Why did it have to be this boy, who loved the people more than he loved his life? More than he loved the throne? This son would never listen to reason. He would never stop giving to the people.

Prince Wendell would lose the throne. He would make

them all suffer.

King Sebastien would find another way.

So King Sebastien said the words, again, that he could never take back. "Get out of my kingdom."

Prince Wendell watched his father. Prince Willis stepped into the room. King Sebastien did not see him until he spoke. "Father," Prince Willis said. "Please. You cannot."

King Sebastien held up a hand toward Prince Wendell. "I want you gone," he said. "Do not ever come back."

Prince Wendell stared at his father for a hundred heartbeats, and then he dipped his head. "Yes, Father," he said. "As you wish."

Prince Wendell took nothing with him. He merely walked from his bedchambers and out the castle doors. His father did not watch him go but slammed the doors and locked them tight against his return. He turned to his son who remained and the girl-child by his side, watching the king with wide eyes.

"You will let him return, yes?" Prince Willis said.

"Your brother has made his choice," King Sebastien said. "He will not be king while I am alive." He looked at Prince Willis. "Or while you are alive."

"But I am a second son," Prince Willis said.

“The kingdom does not know it,” King Sebastien said. “We will bring in a prophet who will spread tales of your magic.”

“But Father,” Prince Willis said.

“Silence!” King Sebastien said.

The girl began to cry.

Prince Willis glanced at her. “What about Clary?” he said.

King Sebastien waved his hand. “You shall marry her when she comes of age,” he said. “She will stay.”

The girl cried harder.

King Sebastien stalked out of the room, without another look back.

Had he looked, he would have seen his only remaining boy take the hand of the little girl. He would have seen the girl shake off his son’s hand and race down the hall, back to her chambers. He would have seen his boy’s eyes turn soft and wet and then, after they had emptied, he would have seen them turn hard. Dangerous.

Just as a king’s eyes should be.

# Quiet

All the children, the king said. Capture all of them, for a magic boy of twelve could turn himself into a magic girl of twelve or a magic boy of seven or a magic girl of seventeen.

There are rules to magic, of course. Rules provide a framework so that one does not find oneself out of control. This rule of magic says that if one were to conduct a transformation spell, one can only become five years older or five years younger, or, perhaps, an opposite gender. One would wear the same face, though one could agree that a five-year-old face is very different from a ten-year-old face, as is a girl's face and a boy's face.

A transformation spell differs from a vanishing spell in its control. A magician controls a transformation spell. But though a magician calls forth a vanishing spell, magic controls its outcome.

So it is not so simple when the people find themselves surrounded by the king's men. The magical children cannot simply touch their staffs, say the incantation, and disappear, away from the hand of danger.

No one in Fairendale is right now thinking of spells, however. The age-old debate of transformation versus vanishing has not even crossed their minds. Not even Theo's, who knows they have all come for him.

Their only thought is, *Run.*

But for a moment, all activity stills. It is as if time has suspended its continuum, as if a moment of such grave danger deserves to be drawn with a slow hand. Only one man moves. Only one man speaks.

It is Sir Greyson. "Please," he says. "Let us do this the easy way. Hand your children over to the king."

But the people do not listen, for they love their children. If only they would listen.

The "run" in their minds becomes a run in their legs. The whole village erupts in an explosion of sound and color and action, all its people fleeing in different directions, screaming different pitches, slipping on the stones so the king's men reach them before they can ever rise.

They run from Death and all the king's men.

Perhaps not all the king's men. For there is one, the one who is called Captain, who cannot trust himself to move. The rain clatters against his armor, and it mirrors so distinctly the clattering of his sorrow inside that he can only drop his head and weep. He must turn away, he must, but he is the leader of these men who slash and slay.

And what about his mother?

Death and the king's men are quick. We could not follow them if we tried. There is a woman who searches the soldiers for her husband, for she would rather hand her daughter to him than the childless soldier who rips the girl from her grasp. There is another mother slain for holding her child close rather than letting him go into the arms of a soldier she knows lives down the street. There she lies broken and red on the ground. And there is her boy, dragged to the edge of the village as if he does not fight with all the strength his little body has, tossed into an iron cage that is waiting for all of them on the wheels of a cart.

It is the same for too many.

In all the clamor, Maude draws Hazel and Theo to her side. "Go," she says. "Go to the Weeping Woods. Meet us there. We shall bring the other children, as many as we can." She kisses them both on the forehead and thrusts them away from her. That is all they need to begin their flight.

But they flee in different directions.

"This way, Theo," Hazel calls through the driving rain and the roaring wind. Her brother moves toward the thick of the battle.

"It is me they want," he says. "I have to at least try to save them." And he is off and away, moving toward a group of tiny children huddling beneath a merchant cart.

"Theo!" Hazel screams, but her brother has already vanished in the rain and madness.

"Hazel!" Mercy says. She is at Hazel's elbow. "We must go. He will come."

They point their feet toward the Weeping Woods and run as fast as they can, without looking back.

If they had looked back, they might have seen more children streaming in after them, flying on Maude's words. They might have seen the king's men give chase. They might have seen another of the king's men, the leader of them all, slumped on the back of a horse.

They might have seen Theo crouched beneath the merchant's cart with a handful of the village children. They might have seen that merchant cart move, barreling through bodies with no place to hide.

They might have seen parents falling, run through by swords and daggers and trampled by the heavy hooves of horses. They might have seen the streets run red.

They might have seen the woods closing in on the ones who made it that far.

Protecting them? Hiding them? Sparing them?

That much cannot yet be known.

In the days after the roundup, the village streets grow quiet. The king has sent his royal custodian to clean them. This is no easy task. There is much blood, though, strangely, the bodies have all disappeared. The royal custodian does not question this, for he knows strange rituals exist for death. He assumes the village people have disposed of the bodies in ways only they know.

The captured children, at this very moment, sit in the king's throne room. Most of them are weeping. Weeping because they lost their parents. Weeping because they are afraid. Weeping because they tried to run, but they were not as swift as the ones who escaped.

"Nineteen," says Garth, the king's page. "Nineteen twelve-year-olds."

"And how many are there in the kingdom?" King Willis says. The number does not sound right. He thought there were more children.

"Forty-three, sire," the royal statistician says. He is a small man, meek and timid with a black mustache that curls around his cheeks. This news of missing children gives him more reason to be meek and timid.

"Forty-three!" King Willis says. "That makes twenty-two missing."

The statistician clears his throat. It is no easy task to correct a king. "Twenty-four, Your Highness," he says.

"Unacceptable!" The king explodes with a violent punch to the arm of his throne. It is a wonder he does not break his hand. The sound is so unexpected that Prince Virgil, who sits beside the king today, startles.

The royal statistician, poor man, does not want to say more, but he clears his throat again. "Also four eleven-year-olds and three ten-year-olds."

King Willis lets out a loud roar. The children huddle together, hiding their eyes from this angry, powerful man with the bottomless black eyes and fiery face and a size so intimidating their hands find each other and squeeze, instinctually.

And then the great throne room falls silent. The

children do not move or speak and barely breathe. I do not have to tell you, dear reader, that silence can sometimes be more frightening than sound.

"Where could they have gone?" the king says. His voice is much calmer now. More kingly. The children open their eyes.

"We combed the streets, sire," Sir Greyson says. He speaks beneath a mask of armor, does not even lift the eye plate. Perhaps he knows better than any that his work is far from done.

"The woods?" King Willis says.

"The Weeping Woods are a dangerous place," the statistician says. He appears surprised that he has spoken. He is not a man who speaks out of turn. He looks at the captain, but it is impossible to see Sir Greyson beneath all the silver.

"We will search it," Sir Greyson says.

"I command it," King Willis says. "The lost children must be found."

"I might lose men," Sir Greyson says. He does not, in truth, know if the danger is worth the risk. To find children who have disappeared? Magic children who might be anywhere?

"Do not return until you find them," King Willis says.

"Visit every kingdom if you must."

Sir Greyson bows his head. "As you wish," he says. He graces the king with another bow that makes his armor clank, and then he strides out the door.

Prince Virgil looks at his father. His father looks at him. "We will find them," King Willis says.

"Yes," Prince Virgil says. His stomach twists once, twice, and he finds that he cannot look his father in the face. He is worried. Worried about his friends. Worried about the children who stand before him. But he must not show that worry to his father, for King Willis would not understand it.

"Now," King Willis says, as if to himself. "What shall we do with these?"

Prince Virgil looks at the children and then quickly away. Some of them are friends. Some of them are not. He does not want to know what will happen to them. He would like to leave the throne room, before this decision is made. And so our prince starts toward the door, but, alas, he is not fast enough.

"Throw them in the dungeons beneath the dungeons," King Willis says.

The children begin to cry out. The whole room is filled with their weeping.

Prince Virgil begins to run. And he is gone before their cries turn to words, pleas, bargains for anything that might keep them from visiting a place that the tales say is a world of dark and cold and rats and spiders and stale bread and sour water and loneliness. Yes, mostly loneliness. It is everything a child hates most.

But what the children do not know is there are people waiting. People waiting to warm them, to hold them, to help them sleep.

One hundred forty-three of them.

They will rock the children to sleep tonight and every other night the dark is filled with bodies.

Even a dungeon can become a home when it is warmed by love.

**Don't miss out on the next Fairendale adventure!**

Will the magical children escape the relentless pursuit of King Willis? Find out in Book 2: *The King's Pursuit.*

## 5 Things You Should Know About Your Narrator

**By L.R. Patton**
**Author**

Since the beginning of time, fairy tales have been passed down throughout the generations. Before written books were introduced into the world, these stories were passed down orally, dictated by a narrator.

In days of old, children would gather near a storyteller, and the storyteller would weave a fine and complicated tale around them as they listened, rapt with attention. And only when the storyteller said the story was over did it end.

Fairendale, you might have noticed, is written much like these old stories would have been told. Our narrator is very much present in the stories of Fairendale, gently offering us her asides on particular happenings, boldly empathizing with the emotions of distraught characters, gracefully shifting our attention to a parallel story happening in the periphery. She is sometimes excessive, yes, but she is, at her heart, a masterful storyteller. I have heard many narrators tell the story of Fairendale, and she is the best for this particular unfolding of events. I trust her completely to tell us the truth, to tell it well, and to tell it with love and honor.

In my time spent recording what this narrator has told me, I have learned some very curious things about her. I thought that you might like to know them as well, so here are a few interesting tidbits about our narrator.

**1. She loves collecting words.**

This narrator has a bit of parchment bound together into a sort of old-fashioned journal. She wanders around collecting not only snippets of conversation and poetry but also simple words. Well, simple and complex words, actually. She is a lover of words and will record the ones that are most interesting, the ones that are most frightening, and the ones that are most beautiful according to her ear and tongue.

**2. She loves sharing her collected words with her readers and listeners.**

Because she loves words so much, our narrator enjoys sprinkling them throughout her stories. She is aware that some who listen to these stories will not know the words, but for this slight problem she recommends searching in a book of definitions and discovering the word for yourself, and I cannot agree more. In fact, I have added a place on my web site (www.lrpatton.com/fairendale) where we can explore the wide and wonderful world of words.

**3. Though some in her life may call her a dark person, she has always and ever been enamored with the light.**

In our world, this would be the difference between a pessimist, a person who always thinks the worst, and an optimist, a person who always thinks the best. Our narrator, though she has seen much destruction and disappointment, is, deep down, an optimist. She believes that stories contain within them enough light to banish the darkness. It is why she tells them so freely.

**4. She can communicate with dragons even when they do not speak aloud.**

Our narrator has many, many secrets, and she keeps them well. One of them is how she could possibly communicate in the dragon tongue—which is a fancy word for the mind-speak that dragons engage in when communicating with one another. She is fully fluent in Dragon Speak. In her presence, dragons do not need to speak aloud for her benefit, because she speaks to them in her mind.

**5. She is a key witness to the drama unfolding in Fairendale.**

You are probably quite curious to know who our narrator is, but her identity will not be revealed until the end of this series. I tried to convince her otherwise, but she is quite headstrong and will only do as she wishes. I suppose, since she is not here right now, I could tell you that she is—

...

I am back. She broke my pen. I have found another, and now, out of spite, I will tell you that her name is—

...

Well, dear reader, I do apologize. It appears that my hands have disappeared momentarily. Beware of telling secrets that must remain secrets.

Now. We must wait until the end of our series to discover who narrates this story.

Thank you for your patience.

Good day.

## A Conversation With a New Student of Magic

**By Arthur of Fairendale**
**Magic Instructor**

The first rule of practicing magic is that one must always be studious and careful. One cannot perform magic lightly or on a whim. One must consider the consequences of magic from every angle. Magic demands energy. It is also unpredictable to those who are less skilled.

How do you become more skilled? With practice.

Of course you can make mistakes. That is why we are here in this classroom. Mistakes are permitted at all times, as long as the student making mistakes learns well from them.

Yes, child, you may interrupt me any time with questions. When you are learning a new skill, it is important to ask questions, so please, feel free to do so. I will never not answer a question.

Now, then. A sorcerer or sorceress does have a limit to his or her magic. Magic is given in differing supplies. Some have stronger gifts than others—

No, we do not know why some are gifted with a greater ability than others. It has been this way since the beginning of time. The differing strains of magic have endured, and it is unclear why some are given ability to practice dark magic along with light magic and some are confined to one or the other.

No, child, you have not been confined to dark magic. I should not have spoken so foolishly. Those who are invited into my classroom are gifted with light magic.

No, we will not learn dark magic in this classroom.

Yes, Maude's cookies are for your enjoyment.

Yes, Maude's cookies will be here every day that we meet in this classroom.

Yes, I know this is my kitchen. But for our purposes, it is our classroom. And since you are a new student, I suppose I should tell you that we meet every morning at half past nine. I will teach you one spell every day, and you will practice that one spell until you master its execution.

No, we will not make more pumpkin spice sugar cookies with our magic.

Here is your first lesson in magic: Something cannot be created from nothing, and once that something is created from something else, it cannot return back to that something else.

What do I mean? Well, I mean that we cannot create Maude's cookies from nothing. We would have to use something tangible—like a shoe or a spoon or a towel. And once that shoe or spoon or towel is turned into pumpkin spice sugar cookies, it cannot turn back into its former shape. Maude would not like that, not when she can bake the cookies herself. She needs her shoes and spoons and towels.

Here are some additional things you must know:

You are forbidden to perform a spell outside this classroom until you have efficiently mastered it.

Magic must be practiced carefully. Undoing a spell is much harder than doing a spell.

My dear, you are simply not listening. Maude makes the cookies. She does not create them from magic. This would be using magic for unnecessary purposes, and that is never wise when it comes to magic.

No, I do not have the gift of magic.

No, I am not rubbing my eye because I have something to hide. My eye simply itches, that is all.

Yes, it is a beautiful day. Run along, then. I see I cannot compete with the view outside this window. We will resume our studies tomorrow.

# The Established Order of the Kingdom of Fairendale

## Powers of the king

The throne of Fairendale is an absolute monarchy, meaning that the king has absolute power of the kingdom. It is not necessary, nor is it required, for the king to have advisors or counselors. If he decides to enforce a new law, it is done. If he decides to revoke an old law, it is done. If he decides that sweet rolls are now considered a nutritious meal, it is done.

## Transfers of power

Transfers of power become necessary if the king is unable or unfit to rule. A regent will step in temporarily when a monarch is ill, absent, or otherwise indisposed. In the land of Fairendale, however, the monarchy has no known transfers of power (these were revoked when King Sebastien stole the throne from the Good King Brendon, who, like any good king, had a very wise regent at his side), which means if the king takes to his bed with a stomachache, he will rule from his bed.

## Order of succession

The throne of Fairendale is always passed to the

firstborn son of the king, provided he is born with the gift of magic. If he is not born with the gift of magic—or if he is a she—the throne can be claimed by any other sorcerer, which is how King Sebastien, a poor boy from Lincastle, became king of Fairendale.

The prince marks his official inheritance of the throne at whatever age the current king considers appropriate, celebrating his succession with a lavish coronation ceremony. King Willis was not coronated until well into his twenties. Prince Virgil, who is twelve, has not yet been coronated.

### Presiding King

Fairendale is currently under the rule of King Willis, son of King Sebastien, who stole the throne from the Good King Brendon. Prince Virgil, son of King Willis and grandson of King Sebastien, is set to inherit the throne.

## The Royal Family of Fairendale

**King Willis:** The current king of Fairendale. Has a deep love for sweet rolls, and it shows in his, well, wideness.

**Queen Clarion:** The current queen of Fairendale. Is underestimated by her husband, but we shall see just how powerful she is soon enough.

**Prince Virgil:** Son of King Willis and Queen Clarion, best friend of Theo. Prefers rye bread with melted butter to sweet rolls, depending on the day.

**King Sebastien:** Deceased king of Fairendale, exception to the line of boys who tried to steal thrones and were, upon failing at their quest, forever banished to sail the Violet Sea. Was killed by a blackbird.

## The Villagers of Fairendale

**Arthur:** Village furniture maker and magic instructor to girls who possess the gift of magic. Is a bit reckless but always manages to come out on the other side—though one is not always assured it will be so.

**Maude:** Arthur's wife. Bakes spectacular pumpkin sugar cookies. Prefers caution to reckless abandon.

**Hazel:** Daughter of Arthur and Maude, twin of Theo. Cares for the village sheep and can even, amazingly, understand them.

**Theo:** Son of Arthur and Maude, twin of Hazel. Finishes his chores early so he can sit in on magic lessons.

**Mercy:** Daughter of Cora, best friend of Hazel. Prefers spectacular acts of magic to "boring" ones.

**Cora:** Mother of Mercy, widow, shape shifter. A woman who moves.

**Garron:** The town gardener. Talks to plants as though they can hear him. Has three sons: 12-year-old twins and a 13-year-old.

**Bertie:** The town baker. Enjoys showing off his air-kneading skills for the children.

## Staff of Fairendale Castle

**Garth:** Page for King Willis, the oldest of twelve children. Sometimes calls King Willis "Your Wideness."

**Cook:** One of the few shape shifters in the land. Shape shifts into a bear. Is highly annoyed by her assistant, Calvin.

**Calvin:** An orphan who began working as Cook's assistant instead of traveling to live with distant relatives in Ashvale—and so did not perish in the Fire Mountain that claimed the entire population of Ashvale many years ago. Tasked with feeding the prisoners in the dungeons beneath the dungeons.

**Sir Greyson:** Captain of the king's guard. Receives

medicine, which keeps his mother alive, in exchange for his service to the king. Carries a magical sword that cannot be lifted by any but him.

**Sir Merrick:** Second in command to Sir Greyson.

## Important Prophets

**Aleen:** A prophetess who is one hundred forty-two years old, from the kingdom of White Wind. Wears ebony skin and what appears to be a collection of snakes for hair (though it is not).

**Yerin:** A prophet who is one hundred forty-two years old, from the wild woodland between Lincastle and Eastermoor. Has white hair that makes the dark of the dungeons where he is imprisoned a bit less dark.

## Dragons of Morad

**Zorag:** King of the dragons of Morad. Lost his parents in the Great Battle, when King Sebastien stole the throne from the Good King Brendon. Would like nothing more than peace.

**Blindell:** Zorag's cousin, raised as the dragon king's son. Lost his parents in the Great Battle, when King Sebastien stole the throne from the Good King Brendon. Would like nothing more than revenge.

**Larus:** One of the elder dragons of Morad, male. Counselor to Zorag.

**Malera:** One of the elder dragons of Morad, female. Counselor to Zorag.

## The lost 12-year-old children of Fairendale

Ursula
Chester
Charles
Thumbelina (known as Lina among the children)
Minnie
Jasper
Frederick
Ruby
Martin
Oscar
Homer
Anna
Aurora
Rose
Edgar
Harriet (known as Hattie among the children)
Isabel (known as Izzy among the children)
Ralph

Dorothy
Julian
Tom Thumb
Philip

# About the Author

While she has never possessed the gift of magic, L.R.'s teachers claimed she had a gift for words, which one might agree is quite like a gift of magic. Bringing a story to life that did not exist before is very much like transforming an old shoe into a dish towel. L.R. feels quite honored that she was given this gift and hopes to use it to encourage other young writers to discover their own gifts, for what is the world without words and stories?

L.R. is the queen of her castle in San Antonio, TX. She lives with her king and her six young princes, who daily give her inspiration for more grand tales of magic and adventure.

www.lrpatton.com

## A Note From L.R.

I hope you've enjoyed reading this book from the annals of Fairendale's history. The world of Fairendale has been a lovely world to create, and I've had fun sketching maps, re-reading fairy tales and thinking, endlessly, about characters and their plights—because a series like this one takes lots and lots of time and hard work. But because it's always been my dream to create a fantasy world and share it with my readers, I knew it was something I had to do. (So, you see, dreams really do come true.)

If you have any questions about Fairendale or simply want to send me a note to tell me who your favorite character is or what kinds of extras you'd like to see me release in the future (a *Creatures of the Violet Sea* is coming soon!), email me at lr@lrpatton.com. I always enjoy hearing from my young readers.

Please consider leaving (or ask your parent to leave) a review of this book wherever you bought it. Reviews help get books into the hands of potential new readers, which is incredibly important for authors like me. And don't forget to pick up your free bonus materials when you stop by my web site! (www.lrpatton.com)

Thank you so much for supporting my work.

In love,

L.R.

# Enjoy more stories from the magical Fairendale series:

LRPatton.com/Fairendale

## Starter Library

## A singular obsession. A safe hiding space. A never-ending search.

The king's guard has been searching all the lands of the realm for the missing Fairendale children. But, alas, Captain Sir Greyson has returned, after many days, to report to King Willis that no children have been found. The king, quite angry at this disappointing news, orders another search, this one closer to home—right inside the dangerous Weeping Woods.

*Continue your journey into the world of Fairendale with Book 2: The King's Pursuit, a short story prequel, "The Good King's Fall" and some important bonus material,* ***free for a limited time.***

***To get your FREE bonus materials, visit ****

***LRPatton.com/goodking***

*Must be 13 or older to be eligible

www.ingramcontent.com/pod-product-compliance
Lightning Source LLC
Chambersburg PA
CBHW030531310726
48979CB00010B/1874/J

* 9 7 8 1 9 4 6 1 9 3 0 1 8 *